THE DREAMERS

Gilbert Adair lives in London and has been regularly
published as a journalist.

by the same author

fiction

THE HOLY INNOCENTS

LOVE AND DEATH ON LONG ISLAND

THE DEATH OF THE AUTHOR

THE KEY OF THE TOWER

A CLOSED BOOK

BUENAS NOCHES BUENOS AIRES

non-fiction

MYTHS & MEMORIES

HOLLYWOOD'S VIETNAM

THE POSTMODERNIST ALWAYS RINGS TWICE

FLICKERS

SURFING THE ZEITGEIST

THE REAL TADZIO

children's

ALICE THROUGH THE NEEDLE'S EYE

PETER PAN AND THE ONLY CHILDREN

poetry

THE RAPE OF THE COCK

translation

A VOID

GILBERT ADAIR

The Dreamers

A Romance

faber and faber

A version of this book originally entitled
The Holy Innocents was published in 1988.
This edition first published in 2004
by Faber and Faber Limited
3 Queen Square London WC1N 3AU

Typeset by Faber and Faber Limited
Printed in England by Mackays of Chatham plc,
Chatham, Kent

The lyrics of 'Que Reste-t-il de nos Amours?'
by Charles Trenet, copyright © Charles Trenet, 1942,
are reproduced with kind permission of
Editions Salabert, France

A CIP record for this book
is available from the British Library

ISBN 0-571-21626-9

2 4 6 8 10 9 7 5 3 1

for Michael, Eva and Louis –
any other actors would have been impostors

THE DREAMERS

The Cinémathèque Française is located in the sixteenth arrondissement of Paris between the Trocadéro esplanade and the avenue Albert-de-Mun. The Mussolinian monumentality of the Palais de Chaillot in which it's housed so impresses the cinephile visiting it for the first time that he rejoices in living in a country ready to accord such prestige to what tends elsewhere to be the least respected of the arts. Hence his disappointment when he discovers, on closer inspection, that the Cinémathèque itself occupies no more than one small wing of the whole edifice, arrived at, almost furtively, by a basement entrance tucked away out of sight.

This entrance can be approached either from the esplanade, an enchanted plateau of lovers, guitarists, roller skaters, black souvenir vendors and tartan-frocked little girls chaperoned by their English or Portuguese nannies; or else along a curving garden path which, running parallel to the avenue Albert-de-Mun, affords one a glimpse, through illuminated shrubs, of the wrought-iron Mount Fuji of the Eiffel Tower. Whatever the approach, one ends by descending a flight of steps to the Cinémathèque's foyer, whose intimidating austerity is relieved by a permanent display of kinetoscopes, praxinoscopes, shadowboxes, magic lanterns and other naïve and charming relics of the cinema's prehistory.

It used to happen that the garden would be invaded by cinephiles three times an evening, at six-thirty, eight-thirty and ten-thirty.

The true fanatics, however, the so-called *rats de Cinémathèque*, who would arrive for the six-thirty performance and seldom leave before midnight, preferred not to fraternise with those less obsessive visitors to whom Chaillot meant no more than an inexpensive night out. For cinephilia, as it was practised here, in the very front row of the stalls, was a secret society, a cabal, a freemasonry. That front row remained the exclusive province of the *rats*, whose names ought to have been inscribed on their seats just as the names of Hollywood directors used to be stencilled on the backs of their collapsible canvas chairs, the *Mr Ford* or *Mr Capra* slightly obscured by the designee's shoulder and upper arm as he turned his smiling, suntanned gaze towards the photographer.

What else were these *rats*, these fanatics, these denizens of the night, but vampire bats wrapping themselves in the cloak of their own shadows?

If they chose to sit so close to the screen, it was because they couldn't tolerate not receiving a film's images *first*, before they had had to clear the hurdles of each succeeding row, before they had been relayed back from row to row, from spectator to spectator, from eye to eye, until, defiled, second-hand, reduced to the dimensions of a postage-stamp and ignored by the double-backed love-makers in the last row of all, they returned with relief to their source, the projectionist's cabin.

Besides which, the screen really was a screen. It screened them from the world.

'Have you seen the King?'

Spring, with its tufts of crocuses and violets bursting forth from nowhere like a conjuror's bouquet of tissue-paper flowers, had come that evening to the gardens of the Cinémathèque.

It was twenty past six. Three adolescents emerged from the metro exit on to the place du Trocadéro and turned towards the path which ran parallel to the avenue Albert-de-Mun. The question had been posed by the tallest of the three. He was muscular and lean but held himself with a lopsided stoop that seemed inconsistent with his physique. Under his jumble-sale clothes one imagined delicately chiselled anklebones and subtle, shark's-fin shoulder-blades. And these clothes of his – the patched corduroy jacket, the jeans whose creases tapered off into baggy nothingness below the knees, the leather sandals – he wore with the genius that Stendhal somewhere attributes to a lady alighting from her carriage. His name was Théo. He was seventeen.

His sister Isabelle was an hour and a half his junior. She wore a cloche hat and a soft white fox boa which, every five minutes or so, she would sling over her shoulder as negligently as a prizefighter's towel.

But she was as far from the sort of mutton-headed misses for whom such accessories represented a fashion statement as would be two athletes running side by side, shoulder to shoulder, one of whom has lapped the other. Not since her childhood had she worn anything new. More precisely, she had never grown out of a childish infatuation with dolling herself up in her grandmother's gowns. She had grown into these gowns and made them her own.

The mutton-headed misses stared at her, wondering

how she did it. The secret was: *she didn't do it with mirrors*. Isabelle would say haughtily, 'It's vulgar to look at yourself in a mirror. A mirror is for looking at others in.'

It wasn't to his sister but to the young man walking beside her that Théo's question had been addressed. Though at eighteen Matthew was the oldest of the three in age, he was the youngest in appearance. He was of a featherweight frailness of build and had never shaved in his life. In his crisp blue jeans, tight 'skinny' pullover and white sneakers, he appeared to walk on the tips of his toes without actually tiptoeing. His fingernails were bitten to the quick and he had a compulsive habit of flicking the end of his nose with his squat index finger.

There was once a faun that came to a mountain pool but was incapable of drinking any water because it would turn aside, again and again, to reassure itself that no hostile presence lurked nearby. It finally died of thirst. Matthew might have been that faun. Even in repose, his eyes would glance sideways, warily.

Matthew was an American, of Italian immigrant origin, from San Diego. He had never left home before. In Paris, where he was studying French, he felt as gauche as an alien from another planet. His friendship with Théo and Isabelle, a friendship which had matured in the white shadow of the Cinémathèque screen, he judged as a privilege of which he was undeserving and he lived in fear that his friends would eventually arrive at the same conclusion.

He was also terrified that he hadn't properly read the small print of their relationship. He forgot that true friendship is a contract in which there can be no small print.

A lonely man thinks of nothing but friendship, just as a repressed man thinks of nothing but flesh. If Matthew had been granted a wish by a guardian angel, he would have requested a machine, one yet to be invented, permitting its owner to ascertain where each of his friends was at any given moment, what he was doing and with whom. He belonged to the race which loiters underneath a loved one's window late at night and endeavours to decipher shadows flitting across the Venetian blind.

Back in San Diego, before he arrived in Paris, his best friend had been a football player, a good-looking youth whose symmetrical features were marred by a broken nose. This best friend invited him to spend the night at his parents' home. His room was in a state of undress. The bed was littered with dirty teeshirts and underpants. A Bob Dylan poster and a college pennant were pinned to the walls. A stack of board games was piled up in a corner. From the bottom drawer of a chest-of-drawers he took out a large buff envelope whose contents he spread over the carpet – creamy-textured photographs clipped from fashion and sports magazines and depicting young men, most of them in profile, all of them in various stages of *déshabillé*. Matthew, confused, believed that his friend was making a confession and that the same confession was now expected of him. So he admitted what he had not realised about himself until that very instant: that he too was aroused by male beauty, by naked boys with nipples like stars.

The best friend was revolted by this unsolicited disclosure. His parents had offered him a plastic surgery operation as an eighteenth-birthday present. What Matthew had taken for erotica was an anthology of sample noses. His heart beating madly, he sneaked back to his own home in the middle of the night.

He determined never again to be caught in such a trap. Fortunately, the door of the closet out of which he had momentarily stepped proved to be a revolving one. Loath to reveal his own secret, the friend didn't breathe a word of the indiscretion.

Matthew began to masturbate – once, sometimes

twice, a day. To prompt the climax he would conjure up images of leggy youths. Then, just as the dam was about to burst, he forced himself to think of girls instead. This abrupt volte-face grew into a habit. Like a child to whom a fairy-tale is read, his solitary orgasms no longer sanctioned the slightest deviation from the prearranged scenario and would ignominiously fizzle out if by mischance he omitted the climactic twist.

There is fire and fire: the fire that burns and the fire that gives warmth, the fire that sets a forest ablaze and the fire that puts a cat to sleep. So is it with self-love. The member that once seemed one of the wonders of the world soon becomes as homely as an old slipper. Matthew and himself gradually ceased to excite each other.

To revive his desire, he constructed a system out of the very gaffe that had caused his heart to beat. Like a good little Catholic, he would confess every week in the English church on the avenue Hoche.

Confession was his vice. It inflamed him more to plead guilty to his petty squalours than it ever did to practise them. The dankness of the confessional nearly always gave him an erection. As for the necessary friction, it would be generated by the delicious discomfiture he felt at having to catalogue the number of times he had 'touched himself'.

For it's easier to confess to murder than to masturbation. A murderer is guaranteed a respectful hearing. He makes the priest's day.

Did Matthew love Théo and Isabelle? In truth, what he had fallen in love with was some facet which was shared by both of them equally, something identical in them, even if as twins they were not identical, something which would dart to one face, then to the other, depending on an expression or a trick of the light or the angle at which a head was cocked.

Naturally, he never spoke to either of the avenue Hoche. He would have died before confessing that he went to confession.

'Have you seen the King?'

'Yeah, yeah, I think so.'

'Well?'

'I don't remember it as anything special. It's not a patch on the Borzage.'

What Théo meant by 'the King' was *Seventh Heaven*, a melodrama made in the nineteen-thirties by a Hollywood film director named Henry King. The same story had been filmed before by another director, Frank Borzage, but it was King's version they had come to see. During the month of March the Cinémathèque was programming a retrospective of his work.

But why should they wish to see a film that, according to Matthew, was nothing special? Actually, it would no more have occurred to them to miss it than it would occur to the reader of a newspaper to cancel his order after an issue of unexciting news. They were not there to judge. They saw themselves, rather, as friends, or guests, of the white screen that would become, for ninety minutes or so, in the manner of an embassy, part of American soil.

As the three of them walked down the path towards the Cinémathèque, they were talking shop: which is to say, cinema.

The conversation of the *rats* was indescribable. Even Matthew, for whom such terms in English were normally reserved for Michelangelo, Shakespeare and Beethoven, succumbed to the cinephilic temptation to describe any half-decent film as *sublime,* any one better than that a *chef-d'oeuvre.* Yet there was something not quite plausible about the way in which the words would pass his lips. He couldn't decide whether or not they ought to be picked up between the ironic pincers of quotation marks, just as someone unaccustomed to dining out will hesitate before an array of knives and forks. He failed to understand that words, like money, are subject to a fluctuating rate of exchange and that, at the Cinémathèque, the *sublime* and the *chef-d'oeuvre* had long since become overvalued currencies.

Only those who have to translate ideas from one language into another will be sensitive to such nuances. For Théo and Isabelle the discrepancy never arose. Hence there was, to Matthew's ears, something truly sublime about the ease with which they tossed these superlatives back and forth, rendering them as light as shuttlecocks.

Dazzled, he was afraid he'd be left far behind, that beside their lyricism his own insipid enthusiasm would strike them as damning with faint praise. So he took to agreeing with them. He made it his role to be agreeable.

If Isabelle was flattered by this attitude, she showed no sign of it.

As a matter of fact, he was agreeing with some remark she had made as they approached the Cinémathèque entrance.

'My little Matthew,' Isabelle at once snapped back at him, 'when two people agree, it means one of them is redundant.'

His face clouded, but he knew he would have to go on agreeing with her. He was like the player who would rather fumble the ball on the winning side than score a goal for the losers.

'I never thought of that before,' he answered helplessly, 'but of course you're right.'

She stared at him. 'Oh God, you're incurable.'

'Stop teasing him,' Théo chided her. 'Can't you see he hates it?'

'Nonsense. He adores it. He's a glutton – no, a gourmet – for punishment.'

Matthew stared back at this terrible young woman whom he loved in his fashion.

'You despise me, I know,' he said.

'*Au contraire*,' she replied, 'I think you're awfully nice. We both do. You really are the nicest person we know. Isn't he, Théo?'

'Don't listen to her, Matthew,' said Théo. 'She's a bitch. She breathes in all the air around her.'

They had just arrived in the Cinémathèque garden.

*

At a first glance the scene confronting them was identical to that replayed there evening after evening at the same hour. But only at a first glance. Something had changed. The *rats* weren't talking shop.

Apprehensive, Théo strode ahead of the others and went to take a look at the Cinémathèque's gates. They were locked. From either side of the padlock a thick steel chain hung in a half-circle, reminding him of the ostentatious fob-watches worn by fat capitalists in Soviet propaganda films. In the middle had been strung up, askew, a handwritten cardboard sign. It read: *Fermé*.

He darted down the stairs two at a time and squinted through the bars of the grille. Inside, the foyer was unlighted. The box-office was unattended. The floor, which hadn't been swept, was littered with ticket stubs. The shadowboxes and magic lanterns, with their paper seagulls, naked athletes and equestriennes condemned to leap endlessly through a ring of tiny metal hoops, sat undisturbed.

Théo looked the way Newton must have looked the moment the apple, or the penny, dropped. An addict denied his fix wouldn't have had a more frightening expression on his face.

*

'*Salut*.'

Théo abruptly turned.

It was Jacques, one of the most fanatical of the *rats*. He had the streaky features of a debauched greyhound. With his long stained suede greatcoat, his bulging shoulder bag, his grimy boots, his cocainy white face and his horrible matted hair, he looked like a scarecrow that the crows had scared.

'*Salut*, Jacques.'

'Say, Théo, you couldn't . . .'

Théo, who knew that Jacques intended to ask him for a few francs, cut him short.

It was a familiar ritual. But Jacques was no ordinary beggar. His petitions were invariably 'to help pay for the editing of my film'. If no one had ever seen this film, stranger things had happened and masterpieces had been fashioned from less money than Jacques must have contrived to scrounge off his fellow cinephiles over the years.

These days it had become less easy for him. Knowing that he regularly rummaged through the litter bins on the place du Trocadéro, one of the *rats* had bought a pornographic magazine in Pigalle and, on the most lascivious of its photographs, scrawled a cartoon strip balloon over the model's gaping pudenda, inside which he had written *bonjour, Jacques* in a spidery hand. On his way in to the Cinémathèque at six-thirty the *rat* had planted it where he could be certain Jacques would filch it on his way out at midnight.

Ever since that incident, which had unfolded without a hitch, Jacques had exiled himself from the front row and would now exchange barely a word with his former friends. Théo was aware of being the only one left whom he continued to ask for money, but he retained an affection for this pitiful creature he had known in better days.

For her part, Isabelle would have nothing to do with him. She claimed that he wasn't clean, that he smelled bad.

'If shit could shit,' she said to Théo, 'it would smell just like your friend Jacques.'

Jacques had shocking news. Langlois had been dismissed. Henri Langlois, the Cinémathèque's creator and curator, he whom Cocteau once called 'the dragon who guards our treasure', had been dismissed by Malraux, de Gaulle's Minister of Culture.

'What do you mean, he's been dismissed?'

'That's all I know,' replied Jacques, who was still angling for an opening in the conversation to borrow money. 'He's gone – and the Cinémathèque's closed until further notice. But I say, Théo . . .'

'Why would Malraux do such a thing? It doesn't make sense.'

'Oh, the old story. The chaos, the disorder, the megalomania.'

Théo had heard it all before. It was said of Langlois that he kept cans of film in his bathtub, that he had mislaid irreplaceable classics; but also that, during the war, he had rescued prints the way others had rescued parachutists.

He was an eccentric curator. His idea of guarding treasure was to pass it around. He liked to show films. He thought it was good for them to be run through a projector. In this he differed from the kind of archivist who believes that projection is harmful to a film – which is not unlike saying that smiling is harmful to a face.

Yet it's perfectly true, projection, like smiling, does produce wrinkles. Langlois's enemies accused him of squandering the nation's patrimony. Films, they said, were no longer kept in bathtubs.

*

Théo, who never read a newspaper, now urgently wanted to buy one. Details, he needed details. Mechanically scooping up a cluster of coins from his pocket, he pressed them into Jacques's palm without first sifting through them. Considering the news he had just received, he could almost imagine he was paying off an informant.

Isabelle was less than thunderstruck by the turn of events.

'I don't believe it,' she pronounced with a clairvoyant's conviction. 'There's been a mistake. Langlois is on the carpet for some minor infraction. The Cinémathèque will open tomorrow. Maybe later tonight.'

She was like someone who hears a shot and tells herself it's just a car backfiring.

'Listen, Isa,' said Théo. 'Take that grisly dead fox away from your ears and listen for once. I'm telling you what Jacques told me.'

'What does Jacques know?'

'He had it from Victor Peplum' – Victor Peplum was another of the *rats*, so nicknamed because of his passion for cheap Italian epics, the kind which feature brawny Macistes and Hercules rippling obscene biceps beneath dainty togas – 'and Peplum had it from one of the ticket collectors.'

'You'll see,' said Isabelle, and she tapped her forefinger against the side of her nose.

The cinephiles had meanwhile dispersed to drink *menthes à l'eau* in one of the cafés bordering the place du Trocadéro. The light in the garden had turned soft, homogeneous, with not the least breeze to disturb its evenly diffused lustre. Enveloped in this half-light – itself raked at regular intervals by another, more concentrated light, from the Seine's left bank, the luminous cone balanced like a gyroscope on top of the Eiffel Tower – the shrubbery had begun to grow shadowy, batlike wings.

Near the Cinémathèque's entrance a youthful couple, incongruously bronzed, dressed alike in grey duffel coats and woollen tam o'shanters, sat enlaced on a bench. Imagine Siamese twins joined at the lips. Indifferent to the world which by popular tradition they were causing to revolve, they repeatedly readjusted the angle of their necks, their shoulders, their arms, like acrobats positioning themselves for a triple somersault. So primitive and unashamed was their lovemaking an anthropologist could have mistaken it for some tribal rite of passage – the mating dance of two tans.

Matthew shivered. The sight of their glowing complexions made him feel whey-faced.

'What are we going to do now?'

First they would eat, on the Trocadéro esplanade, the sandwiches they had brought for the evening.

On the slope descending from the esplanade itself to the Seine embankment someone had aligned an evenly spaced row of Coca-Cola bottles, in and out of which the roller-skaters would slalom at terrifying speeds, hunching their bodies backward like nutcrackers and stopping themselves from pitching head first into the river only by the curlicue of a last-minute skid. Wearing a thin blue vest and sawn-off denim shorts, an immensely tall, slender black shoeshine boy, his own burnished skin the best advertisement for his trade, had put his shoe box aside, fastened on a pair of roller-skates and started majestically to skate in a circle, quite erect, his arms raised horizontally on either side of his beautiful body, in the posture of a crucified black Jesus. Sleek silken hair sprouted from the armpits of the Cross.

They found a sheltered spot overlooking the scene and sat there, dangling their legs and eating their sandwiches.

It was Isabelle who spoke. As a Trappist monk takes a vow of silence, she had taken a vow of conversation. She annotated the spectacle that lay spread out at their feet. She played God.

Insolently staring at a teenage girl with an olive skin, eyes like brown marbles and the inkling of a moustache, she said, 'Now, whatever you think of her, and I agree she won't be to everyone's taste, I simply can't imagine God creating the world without including at least one example of that type. No?'

Or, of a daydreaming youth, blond and bespectacled, the transparent rims of whose glasses tempered a slightly too piercing gaze, 'I daresay I'd have given him finer cheekbones' – meaning, if I were God – 'but, really, the overall effect is not bad, not bad at all.'

Or else, of this amazing pair walking near the fountains – two albino and apparently blind brothers, identical twins, in their thirties, both dressed in exactly the same fashion, both carrying white canes which they tapped in time together, left, right, left, right, as smartly drilled as guardsmen – 'Well! I must say, I'd never have thought of that!'

It started to rain. Isabelle, who couldn't bear 'weather that *touches* me', insisted they take the metro, even if the two boys would have preferred to saunter along the quays of the Seine.

From the metro station on the place de l'Odéon Matthew left his friends and walked back alone to his room in a Latin Quarter hotel, one bookended by jeans emporia, minuscule arthouse cinemas thriving on a Spartan diet of Bergman and Antonioni, and Tunisian charcuteries which for a couple of francs would sell you a lamb or mutton kebab and a gummy pastry with a glutinous honey or lemon filling. The soundtrack of its courtyard was that of a neo-realist Italian film: dance band music, a baby's cries, 'Für Elise' picked out on a poorly tuned piano.

Sleep is a spirit which comes to depend, like most spirits, on the trappings of the séance: the veiled lamps, the drawn curtains, patience and silence. It depends, too, on the sleeper's gullibility, on his willingness to believe that, within a few minutes, if he puts his house in order prior to his departure, he will enter a self-induced trance. Only then does it consent to spew the opaque and terrible ectoplasm of dreams.

Matthew distrusted the occult enticements of sleep.

That night, though, he dreamt. His dream was confused with a memory, a memory of being in London, the year before, on his way to the National Gallery.

He had found himself on a traffic island in Trafalgar Square. Standing on the pavement opposite, in front of the gallery, a young (American? German? Swedish?) boy of incomparable physical loveliness was waiting to cross from the other side. Matthew's eyes welled with tears, the kind of tears which only so extreme a manifestation of beauty will inspire and which, like incompatible liquids inside a test tube, will never mix with shallower ones. He had not the least suspicion of what was about to befall him. For it was only when the boy started to cross the street that Matthew saw his disarticulated limbs. Withered by a neurological ailment, he walked like a slapstick clown, crazily flinging his knees out as he advanced.

The two incompatible species of tears suddenly merged in Matthew's eyes. Racked by pity for this ravishing monster, he wanted to step forward, clasp him on both shoulders, kiss him on the forehead and command him to walk erect. Whereupon Matthew himself would slip away unseen in the crowd, many of whom, dumbfounded by the miracle, would drop to their knees in prayer. In other words, he had a Christ complex, an uncodified psychic category that exists none the less.

That was where the memory came to an end. Now the dream took over.

In it Matthew rushed to the boy's defence against jeering passers-by. He cried out, *But his heart is in the right place!* – only to provoke these passers-by into screaming, *No, his heart is in the wrong place! His heart is in the wrong place!* Then he saw that the boy was perched on top of Nelson's Column, brandishing the Cinémathèque screen as though it were a great yellow quarantine flag. Matthew began to shin up the swaying column. From far underneath, the mob stoned him, urged on by Théo and Isabelle, their faces contorted with fury. He reached the top. In rapid succession the boy turned into Nelson, Napoleon, himself again. On the screen there appeared the trademark of Paramount Pictures: a mountain of snow surmounted by a tiara of stars. Then a shot rang out, causing Matthew and the boy to ascend heavenwards together in an elongated swoon, enhaloed by the Paramount stars like a Madonna and Child by Zurbarán.

A second shot rang out. It was the telephone. Matthew glanced at the alarm clock on his bedside table. He had slept no more than seven minutes. Théo was ringing to say that, after their separation on the place de l'Odéon, he had remembered to buy *Le Monde*.

The Langlois affair was splashed over the front page.

So intensely had the three young people focused their scrutiny on the Cinémathèque's screen, they had remained in total ignorance of what had been taking place behind it. The *coup d'état* had been as well planned as a commando raid. That evening's closure was merely the *coup de grâce*, provoked by the scores of telegrams which had arrived at the Ministry of Culture, telegrams from filmmakers around the world who had donated prints of their films to Langlois and who refused to authorise any further screening of them in the wake of his departure.

From this broadside Matthew retained a single fact, one he formulated in his mind as a theorem in logic. The Cinémathèque had closed its doors. It was at the Cinémathèque, and only at the Cinémathèque, that he met Théo and Isabelle. Ergo, he would cease to meet them.

The shadow cast on the wall by the telephone assumed the shape of a revolver against his head.

'Does that mean I won't see you tomorrow?'

There was silence on the line. Then:

'You mean, go to Chaillot anyway?'

'No, I meant . . .'

Matthew had always yielded to the drift of events. He had been content to let them bear him aloft as, at the end of some ridiculous but moving film they had seen together at the Cinémathèque, Edith Piaf had been borne upwards to heaven on the Montmartre funicular, while the word *Fin* zoomed into the foreground of the screen like the light at the end of a tunnel. In the matter of choosing a film to see, a restaurant to eat in or a decision to make, he had always left the initiative to others. Now, for the first time in their friendship, he would make a proposition to Théo.

'Couldn't we meet in the afternoon? Maybe have a drink?'

The telephone is a keyhole. The ear spies on the voice. Théo, to whom it had never once occurred that he might meet Matthew anywhere else but at the Cinémathèque, realised that he had tuned into a faint signal of distress.

'Well . . .' he replied doubtfully. 'I'd have to cut a class. But – okay. I'll be at the Rhumerie at three. You know where that is?'

His was the tone of someone who gives orders without stopping to wonder whether they will be obeyed, who keeps people waiting in the knowledge that they will wait.

'The Rhumerie? Boulevard Saint-Germain?'

'Be there at three. Ciao.'

The phone went dead. Matthew dragged the quilt up as far as his chin and closed his eyes. His friendship with Théo and Isabelle was a tightrope act. On this occasion he had crossed safely to the other side.

Outside, along the boulevard, he could hear the tuneless heehaw of a police car siren.

Waiting. Matthew was waiting. He had been sitting on one of the wicker seats in the enclosed, dun-coloured terrace of the Rhumerie since ten to three, nursing a hot toddy. It was now quarter-past. That, at least, was the time displayed by a clock on the boulevard opposite him. Matthew, who had slim, brittle, squared-off wrists, never wore a wrist-watch: its buckle and strap against his veins made him feel as queasy as though a doctor were permanently taking his pulse. So he was obliged to rely on street clocks. And he remained so convinced that the first clock he had happened to see was telling the correct time that, even if it was contradicted by every single clock he saw thereafter, he continued to place his faith in it.

Waiting. For the person who waits, Zeno's paradox, which denies the completion of all movement, is less of a paradox than a lived experience. Matthew was living the paradox. For Théo to leave his parents' flat in the rue de l'Odéon and cover the short distance to the Rhumerie (he told himself), he would first have to reach the boulevard Saint-Germain. But, before arriving on the boulevard, he would have to cross the carrefour de l'Odéon and, before the carrefour de l'Odéon, there would be the rue de l'Odéon to walk down and, before that, the kerb of the pavement to step off – and so on, to the point where he must still be standing, paralysed, on the threshold of his bedroom, one arm half in, half out of his jacket sleeve.

As he waited, Matthew watched a group of young Americans strolling past him. They stooped beneath the weight of their rucksacks. With their shawls and kaftans, their moccasins, tinted granny glasses, guitars, leathery water flasks and bewildered children in tow, they somehow knew that they should gather at the intersection of the boulevard Saint-Germain and the boulevard Saint-Michel. It was their reservation. There they blissfully drew on marijuana joints, passing them around like peace pipes. And it was so hard to envisage them in any other *quartier* one was tempted to believe that their charter aeroplanes had landed directly on the place Saint-Michel, taxiing to a halt between the fountain and the Arab touts who dealt hashish from one pocket and discount metro tickets from the other.

It was now twenty past three. The Chinese have a proverb: When you keep someone waiting you give him time to count up your faults. It was typical of Matthew that he should, instead, have counted up his own. For it was, so he thought, his own faults rather than Théo's that prevented the latter from being on time for their appointment. Isabelle, well and good – she crushed him utterly. When in her presence, he would always remember much too late what it was he meant to say. But Théo's superiority was not of a kind to make him feel small.

As it happens, this was only partially true. There were moments, certainly, when he and Théo chatted as equals, indulging in the delirious discourse of cinephiles with less inhibition than was possible in Isabelle's company. But, even then, a spectral Isabelle, so wraithlike as to be almost invisible, would flickeringly take possession of her brother, as in one of those composite photographs in which two profiles are superimposed to produce a third face, one viewed full on, that of a total stranger.

It was the stranger whom Matthew loved. But his love undermined him. He would find himself stammering like a bashful swain in some rustic farce. The simplest sentence became a tongue-twister.

He was still waiting. The elation he had felt when replacing the telephone receiver the previous evening had been extinguished. Here he was again on the tightrope; here it was stretched over a new abyss. It was almost twenty-five past.

On the pavement outside the Rhumerie stood a street musician, a young Moroccan violinist. He was playing, more or less ably, the tune 'Vilja' from *The Merry Widow*. Matthew studied him. Every so often, whenever there was a dying phrase in the melody, he would retrieve it at the very last minute with a twitch of his bow, wrapping it round his instrument like one of those swathes of soft marshmallow which hang in country fairs.

Though he was beaming as he played, he made others melancholic just to think about him. He carried the germ of that melancholy within him as someone may be the carrier of an infectious disease, unwittingly passing it on to strangers without ever succumbing to it himself.

This was one of those moments when Matthew was most vulnerable to infection. He saw himself as the protagonist of the kind of film he detested, a sensitive outcast making his solitary way along sparkling, neon-lit boulevards amid cheerful, bustling crowds moving in the opposite direction. The film's background music would be provided exclusively by buskers, all of them the genuine article, recruited by the director himself in what would have been some widely publicised scouting expedition through the city's streets, squares, parks and metro corridors. And its theme tune – 'Vilja', precisely – would be relayed from instrument to instrument, busker to busker, from the scatty old crone at the Flore, whose grin was as wide and creased as her squeezebox, to the blind Jew's harpist whose patch was the place Monge, as though pursuing him across Paris.

It was half past three when Théo finally arrived, ambling unhurriedly along the boulevard. He wasn't alone. A bored Isabelle had decided to join them. She was dressed in a prewar 'little suit' by Chanel which, ornately cuffed and buttoned, was at least two sizes too tight for her. Since Théo was wearing his regulation corduroy jacket, corduroy trousers and sandals, the two of them gratified Matthew by causing a sensation among the middle-class dowagers with their Hermès scarves and inexhaustible fund of pharmaceutical horror stories who, along with the odd laconic loner reading *Le Monde* or *Le Nouvel Observateur*, made up the Rhumerie's clientele.

Neither Théo nor Isabelle apologised for arriving half an hour late, since it had never occurred to them that he might no longer be there. Théo ran his eyes over the menu and Isabelle, picking up a paperback volume which Matthew had left on the table, flicked through its pages.

'You read Salinger in Italian? Molto chic.'

'I was told a good way to learn a language was to read translations of books you already know by heart.'

'That's interesting.'

But Isabelle wasn't at all interested. She had just discovered a new expression. She savoured it amorously. From now on everything that once had been *sublime* – a film, a Worth gown, a Coromandel screen – would be *molto chic*. Like those devotees of the increase-your-word-power column in the *Reader's Digest* who stake their conversational reputation on the number of times in a single day they find room for *plethora* and *infelicity* and *quintessential*, dropping these words the way other people drop names, she hated to let any amusing phrase go once it had caught her fancy.

It might be a quotation. For example, Napoleon's 'People are prepared to believe anything provided it's not in the Bible', which, though no Christian herself, far from it, she was fond of quoting whether it was apropos or not.

Or else it was a whimsical pet name that would attach itself to an object for ever afterwards. Her cigarettes, which were mauve and Russian and looked like lipsticks, she renamed 'Rasputins'. And if one of them smouldered on after several attempts to stub it out, she would simper, as though impromptu, 'It simply refuses to die! It's a Rasputin!'

Théo and Matthew, meanwhile, decided that they would take the metro to Trocadéro at six o'clock as though nothing were amiss. There was still the possibility, no matter how remote, that the situation had returned to normal. They were hoping to catch fate unawares.

34

A cool, overcast afternoon lay before them.

'We might take in a film,' said Matthew.

'There's nothing to see,' Théo answered. Moodily removing the pink paper parasol that protected his ice cream from the rays of an imaginary sun and shunting its tiny webbed canopy up and down, open and shut, he drew an inkstained copy of *L'Officiel des Spectacles* from his jacket pocket and tossed it over to Matthew. 'Look for yourself.'

It was Théo's practice, on Wednesday morning, when the magazine went on sale, to scribble a star opposite the title of any film he'd already seen. On its every page, as Matthew discovered, there was an almost unbroken sequence of stars.

'Anyway,' Théo went on, 'we'd have to go to a four o'clock show and that means we'd be late for the Cinémathèque.'

Isabelle's derisive voice interrupted them.

'You're mad.'

Théo reddened.

'What's eating you?'

'Don't you realise how ridiculous you are? Both of you. The Cinémathèque is closed. Closed. Going to Chaillot this evening is a waste of time and you both know it. If you weren't such cowards, you'd buy a newspaper and save the price of a metro ticket.'

'In the first place,' was her brother's reply, 'a newspaper costs more than a metro ticket. In the second place, it was you yourself who swore Langlois would be reinstated no later than today. In the third place, no one I know of has invited you to come with us, just as no one invited you to come out with me in the first place.'

His anger at Isabelle allayed by the number, force and serendipitous circularity of his arguments, Théo lapsed into silence and began to fidget with the parasol again.

She stepped up the pressure.

'Oh, I'm coming. If only to see your face when you find out it's closed. What a picture it was last night. You looked as if you were going to blub. Didn't he revolt you, Matthew? Weren't you ashamed to be seen with him? Have you ever known anyone so abject? I'm sorry to say, my brother is just as pathetic as the others. As Peplum. As Jacques. He's a born loser.'

Matthew dared not intervene. He never felt more of an outsider than during these scenes. His silence was that of a pyjama-clad infant standing alone in the middle of the night, listening at his parents' bedroom door,

36

behind which insults are being traded that cannot be taken back.

Théo had said nothing during Isabelle's tirade. Instead, he had tugged so violently on the lever of the parasol that it ended by flip-flopping inside out, like an umbrella on a gusty day.

'What are you saying?' he finally asked. 'You don't think we should go to the Cinémathèque?'

'Of course we're going to the Cinémathèque,' Isabelle replied. 'There's never been any question of not going. What I can't stomach is the sight of you two drooling over the *Officiel* just like your awful chums.'

'So what do you propose?'

'What do I propose?' she said, doing her famous imitation of Peter Lorre. And she leaned forward, speaking in an almost inaudible whisper, exactly as in those film scenes which fade out just as the conspirator-in-chief is about to unveil his scheme for holding the world to ransom.

What Isabelle proposed was this. In the free time that he was able to snatch from attendance at classes and at the Cinémathèque, Théo would draw up inventories of his favourite films in loose-leaf folders which he purchased at Gibert Jeune and which, when they were filled, he shelved in rigorously chronological order. In one of these folders, he would list his hundred favourite films of all time; in another, his hundred best films of each successive year. He had been filling them up since he was ten years old, but there was a film to which he had stayed forever loyal, Godard's *Bande à part*, in one of whose scenes the three leading characters race through the Louvre's salons and corridors in an endeavour to break the record – nine minutes and forty-five seconds – for viewing, or squinting at, the museum's collection of treasures. And it was Isabelle's proposal that they attempt the feat in their turn.

The idea enchanted Théo. It would be a gesture of resistance, an act of defiance against the Cinémathèque's closure. If films couldn't be screened there, very well, very well, they would take them into the streets. Into the Louvre itself. Giggling like children embarked on a private mischief, he and Isabelle tore off a corner of the café's paper tablecloth and plotted the best itinerary.

In vain Matthew advised caution. He was concerned that he, a foreigner, an alien, risked finding himself in an awkward situation if they were caught. He saw himself sent back home to San Diego in disgrace, his studies abandoned, his future compromised. For him the beau-

ty of the cinema was that it confined its insidious poten-
cy to the charmed rectangle of the white screen. He was
like one of those people who visit the funfair as amused
and passive onlookers, all the while secretly dreading
the moment they'll be hustled aboard the roller-coaster
by their more boisterous companions.

But Théo and Isabelle had established a front against
him. Like every couple, in whatever manner conjoined,
they formed a two-headed eagle, now pecking each
other's eyes out, now fondly nuzzling each other's
beaks. Two against one – or, rather, two against the
world – they brushed his objections aside.

'Can't you see?' said Matthew. 'If we got caught, I'd
be deported.'

'Don't worry, little man,' Isabelle replied, 'we're not
going to get caught.'

'You don't know that.'

Isabelle had a reply to everything.

'They weren't caught in *Bande à part* and if we beat
their record we won't be caught either. Stands to reason.'

'Look, Isabelle, it's a fun idea and I really wish -'

'Matthew,' said Isabelle, looking him straight in the
eyes, 'this is a test. Are you going to pass it or fail it?'

And, before he could speak, she added, 'Be careful. A lot depends on how you answer.'

On the place Saint-Germain-des-Prés a sword swallower was performing in front of the Café de Flore. Across the square, waiting his turn to go on stage, a young gypsy, clad in a scruffy Harlequin's costume, propped high on stilts, leaned against the railing of the church. As they passed him, he crossed his stilts as nonchalantly as though he were crossing his legs.

Now too demoralised to offer any further protest, Matthew followed his friends into the rue Bonaparte and down the rue des Beaux-Arts. On their right, as they approached the quai Voltaire, was Degas's ballerina in her rusty metal tutu; on their left, directly opposite her, a statue of Voltaire himself, watching their progress with his wrinkled stone eyes.

Two hearts as light as cork, one as heavy as lead, they walked along the Seine embankment and crossed the river at the pont du Carrousel. As they strolled over it, a *bateau-mouche*, gliding beneath them, its upper and lower decks as gaily lit up as a miniature ocean liner, disappeared from one side and reappeared, magically intact, on the other.

In the distance, just beyond the spruce symmetry of the Louvre gardens, was an equestrian statue, that of Joan of Arc, her chain mail gleaming in the sunlight. Matthew found himself thinking of her charred remains catching at the nostrils with the acrid smell of a burnt-out firework.

Suddenly, without warning, Théo and Isabelle shifted gear into a sprint. They were limbering up for the main event.

Slightly out of breath, they arrived at the Louvre.

'Now!' cried Théo.

They skidded round corners with a leg in the air like Charlie Chaplin! They caused snoozing watchmen to rouse themselves with startled snorts! They scattered groups of tourists on guided tours! Masterpieces flashed past them! Virgins alone or with Child! Crucifixions! St Anthonys and St Jeromes! Fra Angelicos wrapped in gold leaf like chocolate liqueurs! Impertinent, snub-nosed putti plumping up the clouds like pillows and pummelling each other as in a dormitory after lights out! The Mona Lisa! The Victoire de Samothrace! The Venus de Milo, whose arms they broke off as they tore past her, Isabelle ahead of Théo, with Matthew, after a slow start, steadily advancing on the inside! Rembrandt self-portraits! El Greco monks! The Raft of the Medusa! Then, coming down the straight, now neck and neck, all three of them together, for a photo-finish in front of those centaur-like ladies of *La Grande Jatte* who take shelter from the pointillism beneath their frilly parasols!

Not once did they collide, not once did they lose their footing, not once did they pitch into the arms of a watchman. They were miracle-prone as others are said to be accident-prone. And they broke the record by fifteen seconds!

Three abreast, they ran out of the Louvre and didn't stop running until they had left the gardens behind and arrived on the quay, bent double, holding their sides, gasping for breath.

The euphoria of having let herself go made Isabelle's eyes sparkle. She clasped Matthew's neck with both hands.

'Oh, Matthew, my little Matthew, you were marvellous! Marvellous!' And she kissed him lightly on the mouth.

Théo, for his part, had suspected that Matthew would

funk it, that at the last minute he would be caught standing, petrified, at the starting post. Delighted that he'd passed the test, that he hadn't been disgraced in Isabelle's eyes, he extended a fraternal hand.

Matthew, though, pre-empted him. Perhaps because he was still drunk on the capricious animal energies which the race had released in him, perhaps, as well, because he sensed an opportunity which wouldn't soon recur, he raised himself on tiptoe and impulsively kissed Théo.

Théo recoiled. He seemed about to blush, to say something irrevocable. But he was interrupted by Isabelle, who began to murmur in a low voice, 'One of us . . . One of us . . .'

Her brother instantly recognised the allusion. Smiling, he joined in the refrain. 'One of us! One of us!'

Who, having heard it, can ever forget the sinister rallying cry of the dwarfs, pinheads, bearded ladies and writhing, limbless monstrosities at the wedding feast of the midget Hans and the voluptuous trapeze artist Cleopatra in Tod Browning's *Freaks*?

On the horizon, as inescapable as the moon itself, the lighthouse of the Eiffel Tower was already drawing

them into port. Rashers of bacon streaked the sky. Forti-
fied by her nine-minute-and-thirty-second course in art
history, Isabelle mused aloud. 'Why, when nature imi-
tates art,' she said, 'does it always choose the worst art
to imitate? Sunsets by Harpignies, never by Monet.'

An unpleasant surprise was in store for them at the
Cinémathèque. It was impossible to enter the garden by
the avenue Albert-de-Mun. Beneath its leafless trees
were parked the squat granite-grey vans of the paramil-
itary police force, the CRS. Leather-jerkined policemen
lounged on the pavement, absent-mindedly stroking
their riot guns. The barred windows of the vans, as airless as casements in a castle tower, framed the occasion-
al twitch of a shoulder, the only movement visible from
outside, suggesting a playing card slapped down on a
table.

Uncomprehending for the moment, Théo and Isabelle
darted across the place du Trocadéro and headed for the
esplanade. Matthew followed them. Minute by minute,
he felt the exhilaration of the Louvre draining away
from within him.

Not an inch of the esplanade was unoccupied.
Demonstrators had scrambled up on to the fountains to

get a better view of the event and crazily sprayed those beneath them. Others, arms linked, swayed back and forth, humming 'Yesterday'. From time to time a famous face drifted in and out of focus. Wasn't that Jeanne Moreau? And Catherine Deneuve, surely, behind those dark glasses? And, over there, Jean-Luc Godard, a hand-held camera poised on his shoulder?

Dominating the crowd from one of the esplanade's highest parapets was the actor Jean-Pierre Léaud, who declaimed in a hoarse voice the text of a photocopied tract which was also being distributed among the demonstrators below.

The tract had as its title *Les Enfants de la Cinémathèque* and this is how it ended: 'The enemies of culture have reconquered this bastion of liberty. Don't let yourself be duped. Liberty is a privilege that isn't given, it's taken. All those who love the cinema – here in France and elsewhere in the world – are with you, are with Henri Langlois!'

Langlois's name was a signal. The demonstrators waded into the garden and surged towards the Cinémathèque. At the same time, in a cacophony of high-pitched whistles, truncheons erect, metal shields raised in front of their faces, the CRS leapt out of their vans and ran across the avenue Albert-de-Mun, unplayed hands of poker left behind them.

Forced into immediate retreat, the crowd made a confused scramble to the esplanade, those in the vanguard collapsing on to those in the rear, until, frenzied and directionless, half marching, half running, their legs buckling under them like card tables, they backed into the place du Trocadéro and began to spread out along the avenue du Président-Wilson.

It was at the intersection of that avenue and the avenue d'Iéna, where yet another barrier of shields, impenetrable and three-deep, stretched from one pavement to the other, that the demonstration was finally brought to a halt and the esplanade abandoned to its fauna.

Like children who, in awe of its hunting horns, its bottles of champagne, the foxtrots and quicksteps of its horses, the scarlet evening dress of its riders, confuse the hunt with the hunt ball, our three heroes confused the cinema itself with a pitched battle in which the future of the cinema was at stake. They were happy to remain on the sidelines, admiring the actors, applauding the stars. They had no wish to take part. They sought nothing more than to be bystanders, innocent bystanders.

But the film had outstayed its welcome. They left before the end. While the casualties straggled from the battlefield, helped down the metro stairs by those who had escaped unscathed, they were already far away, in long-shot, wandering along the Left Bank, three almost imperceptible dots on the horizon.

In the place de l'Odéon they found the usually routine business of taking leave of each other awkward and affecting. Because the visit to Chaillot had been an extemporaneous shot in the dark, they'd forgotten to stock up with sandwiches. Only now did they realise how famished they were.

'What will you do about dinner?' Théo offhandedly asked Matthew. 'Do you have a gas range in that room of yours?'

Matthew thought of his cramped L-shaped hotel room with its peeling yellow wallpaper and the oblong sheet of glass mounted on balsa wood that, propped up against one of its walls, served him as a mirror.

'No, no, I've got nothing to cook on.'

'So where will you eat?'

The question startled Matthew. Yet he didn't care to remind Théo and Isabelle that of late, after all, he had spent virtually every evening in their company. He hadn't understood that, when they arrived home by the last metro, they would regularly clean out the refrigerator. The sandwiches, the hard-boiled eggs, he had dined off had been a mid-evening snack for them.

'Oh, I can always have a couscous in the *quartier*. Or maybe buy a kebab and smuggle it into my room. Unless,' he added tentatively, 'unless we all go out for a meal?'

Théo turned to Isabelle.

'Want to?'

Isabelle screwed her face in a moue of distaste and said, 'Nah. Isabelle no wanna go to a nasty restaurant in the *quartier* and have nasty couscous.'

Matthew should have known his run of good fortune was due to come to an end.

'I ought to be going,' he said, squaring his shoulders, preparing to be the first to say goodbye.

Théo looked at him, ironically, tenderly.

'Why don't you come back with us?'

'What do you mean?'

'Come back and have dinner with us. Shouldn't he, Isa?'

Matthew instantly scanned Isabelle's face for the most

infinitesimal shadow of vexation that might play across it.

She smiled at him. 'Yes, do, Matthew. It's time you met the folks.'

The implication of her turn of phrase, as Matthew knew, wasn't to be taken seriously. But, like all sufferers from unrequited love, he had ceased to be particular. The words had been said. For that he was grateful. For his nocturnal reveries, for the postmortem of each day that he conducted night after night, it was all that mattered.

'I'd love to,' he said, adding, with a calculated coltish charm, 'I thought you'd never ask.'

He no longer needed a prompter. He was word-perfect.

Théo and Isabelle lived in a first-floor flat on the rue de l'Odéon to which access was gained by a narrow spiral staircase rising from an inner courtyard identical to a thousand others on the Left Bank. The flat itself was large, if one counted the number of rooms, but from any one vantage point it didn't appear to be, since all of its rooms were low-ceilinged and small, made even smaller by its ubiquitous bookcases.

Their father was a dandified fossil, a Giacometti

sculpture in a silk dressing-gown, who lived his life at the edge of a void, but as comfortably as one might live in a villa on the shore of a Swiss lake. As a poet, he was a celebrated perfectionist. Writing verse, he was like a woodcutter who chops down a tree to make a matchstick. To make a second matchstick he chops down a second tree. By matchsticks, we mean words. He was as admired for these words as other writers are for their brilliant sentences.

There were so few words to one of his pages, and so very few pages to a volume of his verse, it was rare for reviews of his work not to take longer to read than the work itself. And, like all poets living above the mêlée and reluctant to descend from a cloud-shrouded ivory tower, he was exceptionally touchy where criticism was concerned. As much scoring-out went on in his address book as in one of his manuscripts.

Their mother was English, a much younger woman than her husband who had cheerfully accepted that her primary role in the poet's life was to serve that crabby invalid: his inspiration. She was ever at its beck and call with an unending supply of placebos – cups of watery Indian tea, vague words of encouragement and, mostly, silence. Once, indeed, when Théo had been stretched out on his bedroom carpet listening to Ravel's *Boléro*, she had put her head round the door so often to ask him to turn the sound down lest his father be disturbed that the famous crescendo had remained at a pianissimo level throughout. As did her own life.

Isabelle entered the drawing room to find her father seated in an armchair in front of an ornate fireplace. She playfully nipped the hairs on the back of his neck.

'Papa, it's us. We're eating in tonight.'

'What about the Cinémathèque?' he grunted, without looking up from what he was doing: slicing open the pages of a book with a bronze paper-knife.

'Closed.' She took the paper-knife out of his hand. 'Can't you see we've got a guest? This is Matthew.'

Shambling to his feet, tugging the halves of his robe together in front of him, the poet contemplated his guest. Having been writer-in-residence at a minor Midwestern college for one unforgettable semester, he wasn't unused to young Americans trooping through the flat, but they had generally been graduate students preparing theses on his work. As he shook hands with Matthew, his eyes appeared to think independently of the rest of his loose-muscled face. He had eyelids like a doll's.

'We invited Matthew to dinner,' Isabelle continued. 'He lives in a nasty hotel without a range.'

The poet blinked. He didn't know what a range was. He thought it must be some kind of American Bar and Grill.

'In that case, I advise you to warn your mother. There's surely insufficient for five.'

Matthew hastened to intervene.

'Oh please, I don't want you to put yourself out on my account.'

'Nonsense, my young friend. We can't have you returning to a hotel without a range. Sit, please. Have a cigarette,' and, plucking one from the pocket of his robe, he held it out to Matthew.

'He doesn't smoke,' said Isabelle.

Smartly retrieving the cigarette, her father replaced it in his pocket.

'Of course you don't smoke,' he said to Matthew. 'Far too young, as I see now. And too young to be living in a hotel, wouldn't you say?' He peered into his face. 'Just how old are you? Fifteen? Sixteen?'

Embarrassed, Matthew answered, 'Eighteen.'

The poet blinked again. He looked at Matthew, suspicion nakedly declared on his features. It was clear he believed he was being lied to. There followed a momentary awkwardness, one relieved by the entrance of his wife. Forewarned by Théo, she insisted that reorganising a dinner for two so that it might serve five instead posed no problem at all.

Dinner was a lugubrious affair. The poet at once launched into what Baudelaire, referring to Victor Hugo, described as 'that monologue he calls a conversation'. Whatever his public, a journalist, a graduate student, a fellow man-of-letters, a young American with whom his children were acquainted, he was incapable of digressing from the script.

'*Hein*, my young Matthew? For, you know, a writer's life is nothing but pretence. What you Americans call "make believe". Do I write a poem, eh? Not at all. Nothing so obvious. I *pretend* to write a poem. I *pretend* to write a volume of poetry. The poet – the real poet, *n'est-ce pas?* – is someone who *pretends* to write a poem, *pretends* to write a book – up to that moment, that miraculous moment, when he finds that a new poem has materialised in front of him, a new book has materialised in front of him. Eh? That is why I will never comprehend the kind of writer – *le genre* Mauriac – who sits down at his table at nine and rises at five. What? Are we in a profession? *Foutaise*! Or else . . . or else it can be compared . . . only just, you understand . . . to the profession of the doctor. You follow what it is I am telling you, my young American friend? That the poet, like the doctor, must expect to be called at any hour of the day or night. *L'inspiration, c'est ça*. Like a baby, it does not choose a nice seemly hour to enter the world. It has no consideration for the poet – *ça non*. But when it does come . . . then, you know . . . it's . . .' – here his voice assumed the reverence appropriate to the pathos of the creator humbled before the mystery of creation – 'it's . . . it's magnificent. For monks is what we are, my dear Matthew, monks who enter literature with our heads bowed, as if taking religious orders. It's as simple as that. The poet for whom the subject, the only conceivable subject, is art itself – and for the true poet, I tell you, there can be no other subject – such a poet is a monk whose whole life coincides with the adoration of his God and for whom posterity is his Heaven. You' – he stressed the *you* – '*you* know what I mean, don't you? The immortality of his soul. For what is an oeuvre, after all, but the soul of its creator? That's why I chuckle so at the antics of those pathetic buffers in the Academy with their pretensions to immortality. *Les Immortels,* hah! Maurois, Achard, Druon, Genevoix, that crowd! What a graveyard, Matthew, *n'est-ce pas*? Dead is what they are, dead, not immortal, dead as writers, mummified as men, propped up in their *fauteuils* like so many old codgers in wheelchairs. What a farce! *Hein*? And, you know, you know, it has just occurred to me, it has just this instant occurred to me, that true immortality, the immortality of Racine, of Montaigne, *qu'est-ce que j'en sais*, of Rimbaud, is to the Immortality of the Académie Française what Heaven is to – to the Vatican. *Hein*? For that's what it is, the Academy, the Vatican of French literature. Yes, but yes, I see it now, the Academy and the Vatican. Doesn't the Academic green rival the Papal purple? Eh? Eh? Don't you agree? Ha, ha, ha! You could almost . . . And . . . and . . . the Thursdays, you've heard of their Thursdays, *hein*, those gloriously absurd Thursdays which they spend grinding out the famous Dictionary? *Quelle connerie*! Is it a French dictionary, would you say? Not at all. It's Latin, my poor young friend, it's Latin. The language of the Vatican. They are *latinising* this sublime language of ours, *hein*? You follow me?'

In his right fist, tightly clenched, Matthew was holding a blue cigarette lighter, one of the disposable kind which can be bought in *tabacs* for little more than the price of a pack of cigarettes and which actually belonged to Isabelle. He had been fondling this lighter, fidgeting with it, zigzagging it every which way over the tablecloth's checkerboard motif. And now, in the silence which followed the poet's concluding words, words addressed to him, he suddenly, jarringly, found himself the object of everyone's gaze.

With a tremor of panic, its lack as yet of any focal point causing it to register apocalyptically high on the Richter scale of his nervous system, Matthew looked up at his host.

'Young man, you must excuse me,' said the poet, sedately folding his napkin in front of him. 'I imagined I was speaking to you. I imagined you were listening. However . . .'

'I was,' a stricken Matthew replied. 'It was just . . .'

'What?'

'It was nothing. Really, nothing.'

'You seemed to be mesmerised by this banal cigarette lighter, facsimiles of which – admittedly, in different colours – must already have swum into the ken of even one as young as yourself.'

He picked up the object, made a cursory inspection of

it, then tossed it back on the table as though flicking a cigarette butt between his fingers.

'Perhaps you'd like to share your epiphany with us?'

'Papa . . .' Isabelle started to say.

'*Tais-toi*. Matthew?'

'Well, sir,' Matthew began nervously, 'I was . . .'

'Yes?'

'It's true, I *was* playing with Isabelle's lighter – the way you do. And, well, I put it down on the table here – the checkered tablecloth – and it happened to fall diagonally across one of these squares. Which is when I noticed it was exactly the same length as the diagonal itself. Look.'

For their benefit he performed a spontaneous demonstration.

'Then I put it lengthwise along the outside edge of the square and I noticed that it extended to the point where this square interlocks with that one. See, that fits too.'

From the table he picked up a dinner plate on which was printed a blue willow-tree pattern. 'Now take this plate. I'm sure . . . yeah, I'm right' – everyone craned to see – 'the length of the lighter is equal to the height of this little pagoda here and its width . . . its width . . . is, look, it's the same as these five steps leading up into it.'

He stared at them all, expectant and flushed.

'It's not the first time I've observed this kind of . . . well, harmony. It's like everything in the world has to share the same limited handful of measurements with everything else. It's as though every object, every *thing*, is either identical in length to every other thing or half its length or double its length. As though there exists a global – maybe even a cosmic – unity of shapes and sizes.'

Matthew self-consciously set the lighter back down on the table.

'That's what caused my mind to wander just now, sir. I'm sorry if I interrupted your train of thought.'

The ticking of the mantelpiece clock seemed to mimic the very heartbeats of time. The poet frowned. For several moments he looked at Matthew with a penetrating but no longer unkindly eye. He cleared his throat, then turned to Théo, who was seated on his left, rocking his chair backwards with his foot.

'You have an interesting friend here, Théo. More interesting, I suspect, than you are aware. You ought to take the opportunity of getting to know him better.'

He turned again to Matthew.

'My young friend, your observation intrigues me. Yes,

yes, it does. For it strikes me as having an application to our own modern society. On the surface all is chaos. Yet, viewed from above, viewed so to speak by God, it all locks together, *it all fits.*'

He waved a hand, one dappled with liver spots, in the direction of Théo and Isabelle.

'My children believe – as, indeed, I did too when I was their age, *n'est-ce pas*? – that the state of – the state of – what name shall I give it? – the state of *rebellious ebullition* in which they live presents a real and serious threat to the forces of power. They believe that their strikes and demonstrations and sit-ins – "sit-ins" is what you say, is it not? – they believe that these possess the capacity not just to provoke society but ultimately to *change* it. What they fail to understand is that our society actually *needs* those disruptive factors which would seem to be most hostile to it. It needs them as a monopolist needs a competitor – to conceal the fact that he *is* a monopolist. And so it is that those who demonstrate and those against whom they demonstrate are in reality just interlocking elements of that – of that transcendent harmony which your little analogy so charmingly illuminated for us.'

No one spoke for a moment. Then the silence was interrupted by a derisive snort from Théo.

'You disagree?' said the poet. '*Quelle surprise.*'

Théo slowly turned to confront his father.

'What is it you're saying? If Langlois is dismissed, we shouldn't do anything? If immigrants are deported, if students are beaten up, we shouldn't do anything? We shouldn't take any action at all because' – he gestured with his arm – 'because, seen from up there, from somewhere up there, somewhere in the ether, everything is a part of everything else. We're part of what it is we're fighting, it's part of us, and anyway it all comes to the same in the end.'

'What I'm saying is that a little lucidity would not go amiss.'

'So everyone's wrong but you? In France, in Italy, Germany, America –'

'Listen to me, Théo,' said his father wearily. 'Before you can change the world, you must understand that you yourself are part of it. You cannot stand outside, looking in.'

'You're the one who wants to stand outside! You're the one who refused to sign a petition against the Vietnam war!'

'Poets don't sign petitions. They sign poems.'

'A petition is a poem!'

'Yes, Théo, and a poem is a petition. Thank you, but I'm not gaga yet. I don't need you to remind me of my own work.'

'That's right!' said Théo fiercely. 'You wrote those lines. And now you reject everything they stand for.'

For a few seconds the poet contemplated his son, shaking his head. Then he turned to the table at large.

'What is the time?' he asked.

Matthew, whom life without a watch had made as sensitive to the time of day as a blind man is to sounds and scents, ventured, 'Twenty-five past ten?'

It turned out to be twenty-two minutes past.

'My dear,' the poet sighed languidly to his wife, 'it's time you and I retired. I have letters to answer . . . letters, *n'est-ce pas*,' he added in a last gasp of his earlier febrility, 'which hang over me like unpaid bills. Stay and chat as long as you like, you three. Why don't you invite Matthew to spend the night here?' he said to Théo. 'That hotel sounds revolting.'

Then he stood up and, followed by his ever-smiling spouse, walked out of the dining room with a gait so machine-like one would not have been too surprised to discover a wind-up key protruding from his back.

*

61

From above, from somewhere in the ether, the check-ered tablecloth resembled nothing so much as a chess-board. Fate was marshalling its pawns, buttressing its defences, plotting its lines of attack. But such an engage-ment can dispense with the convention of alternating black and white squares. It's a game that can be played in the desert, on the ocean. The motif of the tablecloth was merely a private joke for the cognoscenti.

Lighting a cigarette, beaming at Matthew, Isabelle said simply, 'Well!'

'What does that mean?'

'Come, come, little man. Why have you never dazzled us with these philosophical speculations of yours? Papa was awfully impressed.'

'Papa's full of shit,' said Théo, morosely picking his teeth.

'I liked him. I liked them both,' said Matthew. 'I thought they were both really nice people.'

Isabelle, as usual, had a theory. 'Other people's par-ents are always nicer than our own,' she said, tipping ash into the cup of her palm. 'Yet, for some reason,' she added thoughtfully, 'our own grandparents are always nicer than other people's.'

Matthew gazed at her.

'You know, I never thought of that before. But it's true, it's absolutely true.'

'You're sweet,' said Isabelle with a smile that was transformed halfway into a yawn, 'and I'm for bed. Night night.'

Removing her flat slip-on shoes as she made the round of the table, she kissed Théo first then, without any hesitation, Matthew.

'By the way,' she said, half in, half out of the door, 'are you staying?'

'If you'll have me.'

'Goody.'

Théo led Matthew to his own room. The bed was unmade. An upright piano stood in one corner. The bookshelves were stuffed with film histories, directors' monographs and ghosted autobiographies of Hollywood stars. On the walls were pinned photographs of actors and actresses: Marlon Brando leaning with cool pantherine nonchalance against a bulbous motorcycle; Marilyn Monroe standing astride a New York subway grating, her white dress billowing around her thighs like the petals of a fabulous orchid; Marlene Dietrich, the snowy grain of whose flawless complexion could not be distinguished from that of the photograph itself. Piled up on a divan near the door were copies of *Cahiers du Cinéma*. And over Théo's bed – and, by virtue of having been framed by a professional frame-maker, accorded a more elevated prominence than the other pin-ups – was a small oval portrait. It was of Gene Tierney in a still from *Laura*.

Though he had been impatient to know this room about which he had so often fantasised, Matthew was assailed by a sensation of *déjà vu*, by the obscure conviction not only that he had been here before but that something had taken place here of import to him. It took him an instant to locate the source of his malaise. What was this unmade bed, what were these piled-up *Cahiers du Cinéma*, these pin-ups and this oval portrait but, mysteriously transposed, the unmade bed, piled-up board games, college pennant and beautiful faces spread out in profile over the carpet of his best friend's bedroom in San Diego?

It was now after midnight. Plainly, Théo had been hoping to talk shop. He had been looking forward to discussing movies late into the night, lounging on the bed, perhaps smoking a joint.

But Matthew wished to be alone, free to replay, in slow motion, the film of the day's events. So he barely responded to Théo's queries. A naïve actor, he yawned in a conspicuously studied manner, trusting that his friend would take the hint.

At last, reluctantly giving in, Théo accompanied him to the flat's spare room, spare above all in the sense that it was furnished elegantly and starkly, with its parquet flooring, its three straight-backed chairs, its narrow cot and, above the cot, exactly where the portrait of *Laura* hung in Théo's own bedroom, a framed reproduction of Delacroix's *La Liberté guidant le peuple*. A snapshot of Rita Hayworth had been scotch-taped over the face of the voluptuously bare-breasted personification of Liberty.

Left to himself, Matthew lazily undressed and started threading through his mind's projector the unedited newsreel footage he would screen for himself that night. Details already stood out like individual frames scanned by an editor as he holds a strip of celluloid up to the light – Watteau's *Gilles* in the Louvre, the kisses exchanged outside, the shell and shot of battle on the esplanade. Furiously, he tried to banish these fragments from his inner eye. He would not be satisfied with an assortment of highlights. Everything had to unfold in the correct order, at the correct speed.

Absurdly, he crossed himself in front of Delacroix's *Liberté*, recited a dutiful prayer and, wearing only his underpants, climbed into bed. In the semi-darkness he made out the whisper-soft rustle of the curtains at the other end of the room. He closed his eyes. He watched the curtains part. The film began.

Later in the night, when the newsreel had long since run its course, he woke up. At first he had no notion where he was. Then he remembered. Then, as well, he was dismayed to realise that he was awake because he had to go to the lavatory and that Théo had forgotten to show him where it was.

He hurriedly slipped his clothes on and stepped into the corridor. But he had lost his bearings. He was incapable of figuring out the topography of a flat that was a beehive of cells. The first corridor led off into another at a right angle. A door on the left stood ajar. Stealthily, he pushed it open and peered inside. A bathtub, a washstand, towel racks. He switched on the light, walked in and drew the lock behind him.

This bathroom, unfortunately, turned out to be only a

bathroom, not a lavatory. But months of living in a miserably underfurnished Left Bank hotel room had made going to the washstand almost instinctive for Matthew. He turned the cold tap on, raised himself on tiptoe and urinated into the basin.

Back in the corridor he retraced his steps. The air in the house had turned to stone. Straight ahead was a doorway underlined by a narrow filament of light. He padded soundlessly towards it. With a final glance at the corridor, he opened the door.

It was Théo's room, not his own. A pink bedside lamp, left on, threw a pallid spotlight over the bed. What did he see? Théo and Isabelle.

Isabelle was a Balthus. Sprawled out asleep on the bed, half under the covers, half on top, her whole body askew in a pose of rapturous lassitude, her dishevelled head cast back on its pillow, a strand of hair grazing her lips, she was wearing a plain white vest and white panties and looked about fourteen years old.

Beside her, Théo lay naked. He too slept, one leg under the covers, the other free, like Harlequin in particoloured pantaloons, the left leg dark, the right one light. He lay on his back, his ankle dangling over the end of the bed, his head resting on the palms of his hands, like that of someone stretched out in a field. Two curly shadows were visible in the cups of his armpits; the third, that which in the male body forms the apex of an inverted triangle, was concealed by the bedclothes where one exposed thigh emerged from beneath them.

What made them such an extraordinary sight was that the limbs of one seemed also to belong to the other.

For a long, long time Matthew stood stock still on the threshold of the room, transfixed not by the entanglement of bodies in a motor accident but by the enigma of the Androgyne.

Then at last he softly closed the door and tiptoed away.

When he opened his eyes next morning after a fretful night, it was to see Isabelle, as though ready to pounce, crouched on his bedclothes, on all fours, peering into his face. Over her shoulders she had on an old-fashioned woollen dressing gown of a dark maroon hue with, on its sleeves and lapels, corded braiding as convoluted as that which loops the loop on the uniforms of operetta hussars. Just a flash of pastel-pale thigh intimated that, underneath the robe, she was still wearing the plain white vest and panties of the night before.

Matthew had no idea how long she had been crouching in front of him. Nor did she give him time to put the question to her, for she immediately raised her forefinger to his lips and, in a hypnotist's voice, whispered, 'Don't speak. I command it.'

Her tongue protruding, her hand unshaking, half schoolgirl, half surgeon, Isabelle inserted her finger into the soft crevice at the corner of his left eye and slowly excavated the brittle stalactite of sleep that was lodged there. After she had subjected it to a thorough examination on the tip of her finger, she flicked it off, then drew another scabby, yellowish fragment from the right one. If, on her finger, these two incrustations looked quite minute, it felt to Matthew as though a pair of dice had been extracted from his eyes.

When the operation was complete she gracefully slid back into a kneeling posture.

'Good morning!'

Matthew eased himself up on to his pillow. He continued to shield himself with the bedclothes as he was wearing only his underpants.

'What was that all about?'

'Why, my little Matthew,' she replied, 'I was removing the sleep from your eyes. You have beautiful eyes, you know. Théo lets me do his every morning but I wasn't going to pass up the chance of a second helping.'

'What a strange thing to want to do.'

'You think so?' said Isabelle, leaping to the floor. 'Didn't you enjoy it?'

'Was I supposed to?'

'Naturally,' she answered. Then, clapping her hands, 'Up, up, up! The house is alive and awaits Monsieur's pleasure.'

Manoeuvring the train of her robe, she lingered in the room, picking up objects at random and weighing them in her two hands, as though rediscovering some long-unvisited haunt of her childhood years.

Matthew didn't move a muscle. He watched her, fascinated, from under the covers.

Finally, she turned to face him.

'What are you waiting for?'

'Isabelle, please, I'm not dressed.'

She smiled at him, raised her eyebrows as though to say 'So what?' and continued to glide around the room, flitting from the bed to one of the straight-backed chairs, from the chair to a Biedermeier chest-of-drawers, from the chest-of-drawers to Delacroix's *Liberté*, dusting each of them lightly with her fingertips or else lovingly stroking it with the palm of her hand.

Suddenly, at the height of this gala performance, she fired a question at Matthew.

'Who in what film?'

Without a second's hesitation he answered, 'Garbo in *Queen Christina*. The scene where she bids farewell to the room in which she made love to John Gilbert.'

'In the future, in my memory,' croaked Isabelle, imitating the accent of the Swedish actress, 'I shall live a great deal in this room.'

High-kicking a bare leg behind her from under the trailing robe, she opened the bedroom door and called back to him, 'The bathroom's at the end of the corridor, then first on the left. We've got a private wing to ourselves, you know. If you aren't there in one minute, we're coming to get you.'

The door slammed shut.

Matthew had awoken into a state of semi-conscious malaise, one that Isabelle's intrusion had not given him time to identify. Now he traced it to its source. She had just said that she and Théo had 'a private wing to ourselves'. Did she mean a wing of the flat? Could that be why brother and sister slept together in perfect impunity, a Romeo and Juliet star-crossed not because they belonged to two families but to a single one? But couldn't it simply have been solace that Isabelle had sought in her brother's arms, solace from loneliness or insomnia? Couldn't he, Matthew, have misinterpreted the ecstatic demeanour of her body cast every which way, her hands, her feet, those lovely far-flung extremities of hers, connected each to each, like the stars of a constellation on an astrological chart, by milky white limbs in disarray?

In the same bathroom into which he had stumbled the night before he found Théo and Isabelle. They were both in their underclothes. Théo was shaving with an electric razor, while Isabelle sat on the edge of the bathtub clipping her toenails.

Cleanliness is next to godliness as a swimming-pool may be located next door to a church. Innocuous as this little vignette was, it filled Matthew's nostrils with the ambiguous aroma of all the swimming-pools he had ever known.

As a boy, he'd had such a fondness for public pools that he eventually developed into a better, faster, stronger swimmer than either he or anyone else could have predicted of one so frail.

It wasn't really the pools themselves to which he had felt drawn, though he liked to watch their youthful, virile divers, like those delightful statues which earn their living as caryatids or fountains, plunge into the water with the heavy grace of torpedos then furiously set about cutting it into strips like so many pairs of scissors. Rather, it was what took place backstage that had excited his scarcely developed senses. There, with a jolt, he had discovered a cocktail of soap and sperm and sweat, as lithe young men, millionaires of beauty, dandies of nudity, gold medallists in vigour, poise and assurance, would stroll to and fro among squalid cubicles, exhibiting their bodies like mannequins, in the poses of mannequins, in the pose of Botticelli's Venus or Boucher's Miss O'Murphy, on the rosy cheeks of whose bottom one would so like to lay a resounding slap. Nor was it unusual to glimpse, cross-legged, a carelessly draped towel revealing just the skylight of his body, an adolescent Narcissus *in flagrante delicto* with himself, his pose and grimaces making one think of a Samurai at the height of hara-kiri.

*

73

'Here,' said Théo, pressing the electric razor into Matthew's hands. 'Use this.'

For a moment Matthew was uncertain how to respond; and it was by hesitating as he did that he forfeited his chance to dissemble. All at once Théo scrutinised his features, the features of a housebroken mama's boy, as intently as his father had done the evening before.

'You don't use a razor, do you?'

Isabelle slid off the bathtub and approached Matthew. 'Let me see!'

These two white vests, these two pairs of white underpants, one of them bloated at the crotch, the other undershadowed by the dark silhouette of a triangular mound – nothing was more calculated to arouse him, to thrill him to the core, and at the same time to alarm him.

He backed off, only to be pinioned against the closed door, on which a variety of dressing gowns and bathrobes were hanging up.

When Isabelle extended a hand to caress his cheek, he held her off at arm's length.

'Stop it. Leave me alone.'

Brother and sister retreated. They had come to expect docile submission to their banter and teasing. They imagined that Matthew had become immune to it, as they themselves were immune to the boisterous give-and-take of their own mutual raillery. It startled them to confront, in so enclosed a space, his huge, hurt eyes, eyes that devoured his face, devoured the cramped bathroom, craned against its walls and ceiling, its lintels and cornices, like a pair of outsized apples by Magritte.

'All right. I don't shave,' he answered sulkily. 'What of it?'

'Nothing,' murmured Isabelle, smirkingly contrite.

'My father was the same,' he went on. 'He didn't shave till he was in his twenties. It's not uncommon.'

'Of course not. It's just . . .'

'What?'

'Unusual for an American, no?' said Isabelle. 'More like a Mexican.'

'A Mexican?'

'A Mexican Hairless.'

'What's a Mexican Hairless?'

'It's a dog,' said Isabelle. 'And what's interesting about it is that it isn't hairless at all. It has hair where people have hair. The question is, have you?'

'What?'

'Have you hair . . . there?'

Without embarrassment, she indicated the spot on her own body.

Love is blind but not deaf.

Matthew felt his lower lip tremble. In a moment or two it would have dissolved into a nerveless, blubbery pat of redcurrent jelly. His mouth awash with tooth-paste and water, he abruptly left them.

Walking along the corridor back to the spare room, he could hear a quarrel erupt between Théo and Isabelle, then the slamming of a door. Out of breath, still in his underclothes, rubbing his chin with a towel, Théo caught up with him.

'Don't take it so seriously,' he said, sliding his arm about Matthew's shoulders. 'It's nothing to what I get every day of my life.'

'Too late. I'm leaving.'

'Leaving? You haven't had breakfast yet.'

'I never eat breakfast.'

'But we were going to invite you to stay on.'

'What?'

'Our parents are off tomorrow to Trouville. For a month. And we thought you might like to move your things here. You don't have to return to that room of yours, do you? You haven't paid up in advance?'

'No . . .'

'Well, stay. Isa will be disappointed if you don't. We talked it over last night.'

That was a slip of the tongue. Since, on the evening before, Isabelle had risen from the table first, she and Théo shouldn't have been able to communicate with each other until morning. But Matthew's mind had begun to dwell on arguments less petty and more potent.

He had been offered privileged access to a secret world, a world from which he had always been excluded, a planet far from the solar system of average, upright citizens who, like mediaeval astronomers, tend to confuse that solar system with the universe itself. It was a world of which he had known nothing a mere twenty-four hours earlier. Its inhabitants he had frequented only when it had taken their fancy, like Caliphs or angels, to roam incognito through the ordinary world of average, upright citizens.

This planet, orbiting as it did around the place de l'Odéon, already boasted entangled legs, unmade beds, a communal bathroom that was warm, moist, dewy-windowed and redolent of suspect odours, as well as other mysteries which remained as yet unveiled but might be made accessible in their turn.

To take up residence in the flat, for however brief a spell, would be a mistake: that he surely knew. Not to take up residence would be no less of a mistake. The thing was to make the right mistake, not the wrong one.

When Isabelle came to grace his forehead with a prim, sisterly kiss and apologise, with what certainly sounded like sincerity, for her callousness, Matthew said yes. They would collect his belongings from the hotel room later that day.

It transpired that the flat did after all contain a wing of sorts, one inhabited exclusively by the young people. They had even given it a name: *le quartier des enfants*. On Matthew's way to the kitchen, where all three of them sat with elbows on the table and dunked buttered tartines into their bowls of coffee, he realised how far from the centre of the household their bedrooms were.

Since he had always had too fragile a constitution to have been packed off to summer camp as a child, and thus had never known the experience of breakfasting outside his own family circle, Matthew was determined to preserve the memory of that very first morning as, in its pristine state, unwrinkled by projection, one preserves the negative of a film. But his determination ended by investing each of his gestures with an unwarranted solemnity. Like Queen Christina, he felt he was touching that coffee bowl, that spoon, that sugar shaker, for the last rather than the first time.

It rained all day and the three friends stayed indoors. Having withdrawn early to his study to tend his inspiration, the poet manifested no further interest in Matthew's welfare. His wife had gone shopping for the trip to Trouville.

The boys spent the day lounging about Théo's bedroom as bonelessly as cats, chatting, devising movie quizzes with which to test each other's memory, bringing Théo's albums up to date.

Isabelle, for her part, had no patience with their infantile pastimes. She read a novel by Queneau, voraciously turning its pages as though the foot of every page heralded some stunning reversal whose consequence would only be divulged at the top of the next. From time to time, she uncoiled her angular limbs, stretched over to a small record-player on the carpet and set its needle down on a record, invariably the same scratchy number, Charles Trenet's *'Que reste-t-il de nos amours?'*, to which she was addicted.

> *Ce soir le vent qui frappe à ma porte*
> *Me parle des amours mortes*
> *Devant le feu qui s'éteint.*
> *Ce soir c'est une chanson d'automne*
> *Devant la maison qui frissonne*
> *Et je pense aux jours lointains.*
>
> *Que reste-t-il de nos amours?*
> *Que reste-t-il de ces bons jours?*
> *Une photo, vieille photo*
> *De ma jeunesse.*
>
> *Que reste-t-il des billets-doux,*
> *Des mois d'avril, des rendezvous?*
> *Un souvenir qui me poursuit*
> *Sans cesse.*
>
> *Bonheurs fanés, cheveux aux vents,*
> *Baisers volés, rêves mouvants,*
> *Que reste-t-il de tout cela?*
> *D^tes-le-moi.*

> *Un p'tit village, un vieux clocher,*
> *Un paysage si bien caché,*
> *Et dans un nuage le cher visage*
> *De mon passé.*

When Isabelle stirred herself to play the song yet again, for what must have been the ninth or tenth time, her brother glared at her.

'If I have to listen to that record once more, I swear I'll break it in two.'

Isabelle's eyes opened wide in amazement.

'You like Charles Trenet.'

'Wrong. I used to.'

'Listen to him, Matthew. Théo's seen *Laura* eight times – eight times, can you imagine? And he orders me to stop playing one little record. Well, I won't.'

Attempting to feign nonchalant unflappability, she set the needle back down.

After the statutory crackly hiss, the record clearing its throat, Trenet's voice rang out.

> *Ce soir le vent qui frappe à ma porte*
> *Me parle des amours mortes*
> *Devant le feu qui s'éteint.*

Théo galvanised his long lazy frame into life and Isabelle at once installed herself in front of the record-player to shield it from him. A clash of arms seemed inevitable. Then:

> *Que reste-t-il des billets-doux,*
> *Des mois d'avril, des rendezvous?*
> *Un souvenir qui me poursuit . . .*
> *Un souvenir qui me poursuit . . .*
> *Un souvenir qui me poursuit . . .*

The needle had stuck.

Instead of appeasing Théo's rage, the accident fuelled it. Striving to push him away with her fists, Isabelle protested in a high, girlish shriek.

'Stop it, stop it! Wait! Matthew, tell me. What film?'

'What?'

Isabelle was still trying to fend off Théo.

'Name a film – *arrête, je te dis!* – name a film in which a needle gets stuck in a record. Forfeit to pay if you can't answer.'

'A needle gets stuck in a record?'

'Quick, quick, or you pay the forfeit!'

Matthew racked his memory and finally trumpeted, '*Top Hat!*'

'*Top Hat?*'

'Remember? Fred Astaire is tap-dancing in his hotel room above Ginger Rogers' suite and the record sticks?'

Isabelle reflected for a few seconds, trying to summon a mental image of the scene.

'He's right, you know,' said Théo.

'Then bravo, my little Matthew!' Isabelle cried.

'But, Isabelle, what would the forfeit have been?'

'Ah,' said she, 'that would be telling.'

And that was how the game began.

Isabelle, for whom everything had to be given a name, even those things that need no names, christened it Home Movies. The idea was this: they would be calmly going about their business, together or separately, reading, playing backgammon in front of the fire, assigning stars to the films listed in *L'Officiel des Spectacles* – it tended to be the most humdrum of occupations – when one of them, besieged without premeditation by some idle memory, would come to a halt, re-enact a snippet of *mise en scène* for the benefit of the other two and call out 'What film?' or 'What scene?' or else 'Name a character who . . .'

Later that same day, for example, filing newspaper cuttings he had been accumulating for years, Théo placed a glass paperweight – the type which, inverted, produces a miniature snowstorm – on top of them. Then, with a reckless sweep of his shoulders, perhaps deliberate, perhaps not, he knocked it on to the carpet. Without even giving him an opportunity to pose the prescribed question, Matthew and Isabelle cried out in unison, *'Citizen Kane!'*

That was an easy one. But, with time, the game became more and more difficult. On another morning, in the kitchen, this exchange could be heard between Matthew and Théo.

'Théo, I wonder –'

'Matthew, would you –'

A pause, then:

'Go ahea -'

'Sorry. What was –'

A further pause.

'I just want –'

'I meant to –'

It was then that Matthew pounced.

'Name a film!'

'What?'

'Come on, Théo. Name a film, just one film, in which two people keep trying to speak at the same time.'

What ensued were mingled protestations of 'Don't tell me, don't tell me!' and 'Time's up! Forfeit!' – until Théo either named the film or paid the forfeit.

The forfeits had, to start with, a strictly monetary basis. A franc, two francs, fifty centimes, depending on the victim's resources and the victor's whim. But they would rapidly grow bored with such trifling prizes, which, in truth, as their meagre funds were eventually to be pooled, came to seem all very pointless. No, just as a hierarchy of trials, ordeals and challenges would transform this game, one that had started so harmlessly in childish pranks and giggles, into a sacrament and a liturgy, so, in their turn, would its forfeits acquire an entirely new significance.

Let's return to that first afternoon. Théo and Matthew left the flat at five o'clock. Théo's mobylette stood padlocked and chained at the foot of the stairs in the apartment building's hallway. The plan was that he would ride to the hotel with Matthew on the pillion seat, deposit his passenger in front of it and return home, leaving Matthew to pack his bags and make his own way back to the flat in a taxi. But there would be a detour in his itinerary, one he hadn't dared divulge to

Isabelle, for he intended to take a turn round the Cinémathèque to see whether, by chance, it had reopened its doors. Fearing his sister's viperish tongue, he swore Matthew to secrecy on pain of torture.

Yet someone who entreats you not to divulge a confidence will almost certainly blurt it out again before you do. So it proved here. So quickly, indeed, that by the time Matthew re-entered the *quartier des enfants*, Isabelle was already privy to a secret which not even the rack would have drawn from his own lips. Need it be said, the *Fermé* sign was still attached to the Cinémathèque grille.

Matthew, too, had his secret. It was Tuesday, the day on which he was accustomed to go to confession. Which is why, after Théo had sped away, he walked off in the opposite direction from his hotel and took the metro to the avenue Hoche.

There, in the English church, in an alcove directly facing the confessional, stood a plaster Madonna with a globe of the world, like a basketball, clutched in her hands over the sculpted folds of her robe. Her pale head tilted to one side. Her halo, ringed by a garland of stars, resembled an electric fan in motion. Her glazed, unfocusing eyes were open but looked closed, as though

86

false pupils had been pencilled on to the surface of her eyelids.

Matthew knelt before her and prayed for something which it isn't regarded as proper to pray for, something which, if ever it came to pass, he would be compelled to confess and repent.

In vain he struggled with himself not to articulate, even wordlessly, his blasphemous appeal. Alas, the trouble with the flesh is not that it's weak but that it's strong.

In fact, the Virgin heard his prayer. And even if her painted eyes did not shed any tears, Matthew's did – which is itself a kind of miracle.

Walking back along the aisle, he noticed an elderly woman leaving the confessional booth. After a moment of hesitation, he entered it in his turn.

'Bless me, Father,' he mumbled, 'for I have sinned.'

The priest's accent was Irish, his voice weary and sonorous.

'How long is it since you've been to confession?'

'You don't understand, Father,' said Matthew, impatient to be done with it. 'I've *just* sinned. Right here in your church.'

'Eh?' said the dozy priest, who had abruptly snapped out of his torpor.

Back at the hotel Matthew stuffed his belongings into a leather suitcase. Then he paid his bill and had the receptionist ring for a taxi.

When his taxi stopped at traffic lights near the carrefour de l'Odéon, a fire engine went storming past, its siren wailing, its massive hosepiping coiled like braided hair, its scarlet-clad firemen clinging on for dear life like the Keystone Kops. Its appearance made him think of his bedroom in San Diego, of his parents' house, of their neighbours' houses all alike in having sprinklers on their lawns and beige-and-cream station wagons parked outside their open garage doors. For there is something cosy, unexpectedly conducive to nostalgia, about a fire engine.

He looked away again. The lights turned to green and the taxi drove off.

That evening Matthew dined with Théo and Isabelle in a seafood brasserie on the place Bienvenue in Montparnasse. It was his treat for having been invited to stay at the flat. They ordered a colossal platter of oysters, mussels, crayfish, whelks, shrimp, crab and lobster, all nestling on a bed of crushed ice. Plying hammers, pincers and tongs, they left the plate as devastated as an archaeological dig.

It was a few minutes after midnight when they returned to the flat. The poet and his wife had already retired. Their plan was to set out for Trouville at the crack of dawn.

Not infrequently, when about to begin or end one of his books, the poet chose in this way to decamp to his summer house on the Normandy coast. And though, on earlier trips, when his children were children, his wife had remained in Paris, her presence was now required at his side, should ever, at some eternal twenty-past or twenty-to the inspirational hour, the capricious guardian angel of his Muse decline to alight on the virgin page.

The children, he insisted, could be trusted on their own. They were mature, intelligent beings. Besides, there was his sister, a maiden lady in her early sixties, to ensure that all was as it should be.

And, time and time again, he would be proved right. He and his wife would arrive back to find the flat in shipshape order, their offspring conscientiously engaged on homework, translating Virgil or working out some mathematical puzzle involving pipes, wash basins and dripping taps.

Unguessed, undreamt of, was the metamorphosis which the flat and its occupants had meanwhile undergone. For each such departure of their parents would leave the two young people to their own devices. Many, various and wonderful were these devices, and both Théo and Isabelle, at least since their adolescence, would avail themselves of the physical and spiritual freedom vouchsafed them. Like gamblers who, deprived of their cards or dice, will bet on car registration numbers, on the speed at which raindrops slither down a window pane, on anything at all, they needed nothing but a mutual, unconditionally offered complicity to descend to their private shades.

Venturing into the world at large, they dipped their lights as a car will dip its headlamps when encountering another on a nocturnal highway. Thereafter, when once the door to the world had closed behind them, these same lights would blaze out brightly, blinding the naked eye.

What was to happen, then, was not a new occurrence; if their folly this time was more acute, it was maybe that

in Matthew they had at last found a child for their inces-
tuous cradle.

The first few days were uneventful. Every morning, in
the kitchen, they breakfasted on cold cereal, undaunted
by the fragments of dried cornflakes with which the
sides of their unrinsed bowls would become encrusted.
Then Isabelle would accompany her brother on his
mobylette to the lycée which both of them attended,
while Matthew took the metro to his own school in the
suburbs. Every evening, on their return, shedding over-
coats, jackets and scarves over the hallway floor, they
withdrew into the *quartier des enfants* and gave themselves up to the increasingly compulsive sessions of
Home Movies, for which they had now started to keep a
score.

These were blissful days for Matthew, who would
sometimes, on his way back from school, travel by
metro no further than Denfert-Rochereau. From there,
with a springing step, he would walk the remaining distance to the flat, titillating himself with the prospect of
spending yet another evening in the company of his
beloved mentors and tormentors.

Inevitably, though, things couldn't last too long as

they were. For this is how a drug works. It ensnares its victim with the finesse of a card-sharp, letting the future addict win a few hands before moving in for the kill. Théo and Isabelle were born addicts, addicts to whose cravings the cinema and each other were the sole opiates ever to have presented themselves. And Matthew – who, had he not left San Diego, would doubtless have married some childhood sweetheart, some winsome flirt, all patience, gratitude and guile – Matthew had once and for all pledged himself to their unstable fortunes.

The first phase of Home Movies, its prehistory, was therefore of fairly short duration, and it wasn't long before Isabelle, exasperated by having to wait for chance to strike unbidden, decided to force the issue.

One afternoon, wearing white overalls, an improvised white turban and a pair of white-rimmed dark glasses, like some thirties Hollywood actress snapped in a relaxed pose on the veranda of her Bel Air mansion, she looked into Théo's bedroom, where he and Matthew were reading aloud to each other from back numbers of *Cahiers du Cinéma*. Her beady eyes registered the mounting clutter of books, magazines, underclothes, half-consumed sandwiches and peanut shells. Smiling to herself, she took a cigarette and tapped one end of it against the pack with clipped, staccato violence. Then, with an ostentatious puff, chewing the remark in the corner of her mouth as though it were a wad of bubble gum, she spat out, 'What a dump!'

Without raising his eyes from the page, Théo mechanically called back, 'Liz Taylor in *Who's Afraid of Virginia Woolf.*'

Isabelle beamed in triumph.

'Wrong!'

'I am not!'

'Yes you are!'

'In the opening scene of *Who's Afraid of Virginia Woolf* –'

Realising his mistake, he broke off.

'Oh, I get it. She's imitating someone else, isn't she? Bette Davis?'

'In what, brother dear?'

'God, I should know this. Is it a film I've seen?'

'We saw it together.'

'We did?'

He thought hard.

'Give me a clue.'

'Certainly not.'

'Be a sport. The director's name.'

'No.'

'Just the director's name.'

'No.'

'The number of words in the title.'

'I said no.'

'The number of words in the title? Is that asking so much?' He started to wheedle. '*S'il te plaˆt,* Isa, *s'il te plaˆt.*'

'No.'

'The first letter of the first word.'

'God, you're pathetic,' Isabelle said with a sneer. 'Isn't he pathetic, Matthew? Don't you think he's pathetic?'

'Matthew!' Théo cried. 'I bet you know!'

But Isabelle quickly put an end to that. Had the Sphinx given Oedipus a clue?

Théo was forced to concede defeat.

'*Beyond the Forest,*' said Isabelle. 'Directed by King Vidor. 1949.' Then: 'Forfeit.'

'Okay. How much?'

'Not this time,' she replied, still imitating Bette Davis. 'This time I want to be paid in kind.'

'How do you mean, paid in kind?'

Isabelle lowered her movie-star glasses down the bridge of her nose.

'I dare you to do now, in front of us, what I've watched you do' – she removed the glasses altogether and waved them in the direction of the oval portrait of Gene Tierney – 'in front of her.'

This challenge – mystifying to Matthew, who could none the less sense the hovering play of strange new shadows about the room – was met with a silence so absolute it was more than capable of holding its own amidst all manner of extraneous, earthbound sounds. In vain Trenet's voice attempted to interrupt it.

> Ce soir c'est une chanson d 'automne
> Devant la maison qui frissonne
> Et je pense aux jours lointains.
>
> Que reste-t-il de nos amours?
> Que reste-t-il de ces bons jours?
> Une photo, vieille photo
> Da ma jeunesse.

Glancing first at Matthew, Théo then turned once more to his sister, his mouth disfigured by a hard ball of sullenness.

'I don't know what you're talking about.'

'Oh yes you do, my pet,' Isabelle continued suavely.

'Only, *voilà*, you didn't know I knew. Those afternoons when you come home from school and you bolt your door and the bedsprings start to jangle – good grief, do you fancy I'm too thick to guess what's going on? Besides, your bed is directly opposite the keyhole.'

Bonheurs fanés, cheveux aux vents,
Baisers volés, rêves mouvants,
Que reste-t-il de tout cela?
Dˆtes-le-moi.

Un p'tit village, un vieux clocher . . .

'Forfeit,' Isabelle repeated calmly.

'I won't do it.'

'Won't do it?'

'You wouldn't.'

Isabelle grinned. Looking up at the portrait, she said, 'Gene Tierney isn't my type.'

'What a bitch you are. A bitch and a sadist.'

'No, I'm a Sadian. Not quite the same thing.' She yawned. 'Are you going to pay the forfeit or chicken out – which, you realise, will mean the end of the game?'

Théo's eyes took in each of them in turn – Isabelle, Matthew, the oval portrait.

'Very well, Isa. The game must go on.'

He spoke in the voice of an actor who receives a fateful telegram just as the curtain is about to rise on some smart drawing-room comedy.

Matthew had never found himself closer to detesting Isabelle than at this instant. He detested her for having exacted from Théo, from his friend, a humiliating covenant of whose precise nature he remained as yet in ignorance but which already evoked uneasy memories of indignities inflicted by leering Boy Scouts in tents pitched in lonely glades.

Yet we are most merciless when we discover our own baseness, our own wretched hypocrisies, reflected in another's, and the dread which swept over him, a dread encompassing not only Théo's but his own future on this island, this planet, in this first-floor flat off the place de l'Odéon, was coupled with an almost uncontrollable exhilaration.

Théo stood up and took off his sweater. Unbuttoning his shirt, he drew it back over his shoulder-blades. His chest was hairless except for a single dark wisp which sprang from his navel like a mountain stream before plunging underground beneath his trouser belt. Unbuckling the belt, he let his corduroy jeans crumple

97

to his feet. Then, bending forward, he jerked them free.

Whereupon, Isabelle clapped her hands over her eyes and shrieked, 'No, no! For the love of God, no!'

Matthew was astonished. Was she having second thoughts? Did she realise that Théo had outsmarted her by calling her bluff?

Hardly. For, peeking gingerly through her interlocked fingers as through two slats in a blind, she shuddered.

'How often have I told you never to take your trousers off before your socks! Look at yourself, you half-wit, you've got navy blue socks on. They give you that ghastly truncated look when you're naked. Take them off at once.'

Scowling at his sister, Théo tugged off his socks. After a pause, he began to remove his white underpants, rolling rather than drawing them over his sexual organs the way a woman will roll back a nylon stocking before inserting her foot in its sheath and smoothing it out along her leg with the flat of her hand. Then he flipped them about his ankles and stood before them, knees together, shivering slightly, like some arrowless Sebastian.

Now that he was free of the grubby chrysalis of his own clothes, the transformation was as startling as with those raggedy street urchins of Fez or Tangiers who, once on the beach, moult into the finery of their nakedness.

He stood for a second or two contemplating his penis. It was almost erect. His testicles looked as heavy as gourds.

He knelt on the bed beneath the oval portrait. His eyes captivated by the mask of imperturbability with which the actress requited their gaze, he started to massage himself. Paced by the rhythm of the bedsprings, which reverberated through the room like the pistons of an express train carrying him closer and closer to his goal, his hand went faster and faster, instinctively rediscovering its old familiar pulsation. It was as though his livid member were steering his hand's movements, not vice versa, as though he wouldn't have been capable of unprising his fingers from it even had he wished to, the way, for a single frightful moment, one's fingers stick fast to the scalding handle of a saucepan. And when the climax arrived, the jet of sperm that his penis discharged, sperm glistening, so it appeared to Matthew, with tiny, pearly scintillae of light, hovered in the air for a split second, arrested in flight, like a fountain that all of a sudden freezes over, producing, at the snap of one's fingers against the sparkling little pinnacle of ice that it has become, a high, pure, silvery musical note.

Then, brusquely, all was damp stickiness, matted hair on the thighs, the faint, sweetish odour of fish paste.

Théo lay back on the bed, panting, propped up on one side, his hands aligned along the ridge of his spine, in the posture of an opium smoker. In the bird's nest of his crotch the mother bird once more placidly nursed her two eggs.

Isabelle was a subtle voyeur. She liked to spy on voyeurs. Behind her dark glasses, while Théo masturbated, her eyes had nervously darted to and fro, from her brother to Matthew and back again. Now, the performance over, those eyes had become indecipherable. Only a flutter of eyelashes could be discerned behind their shades, as of moths in the night.

As for Matthew, who had watched the scene without saying a word, his body could no more lie about his feelings than he himself could. His cheeks were inflamed, his hands shook, his crotch felt like a clenched fist between his thighs. He wondered how he could ever face Théo again.

*

Most unexpectedly, though, from this raising of the stakes there followed a truce, an armistice, one that was to see them through the following two days. Whether because nothing that any of them said or did would conjure up a matching gesture in some classic film or, more likely, because it impressed them all as equally unimaginable either to advance or retreat, the cry of 'What film?' or 'Name a film' ceased for a while to echo through the flat.

Matthew knew that the matter hadn't ended, couldn't end, there. To be sure, Théo had clothed himself again without fuss and afterwards acted as though nothing had occurred to occasion any change of policy. But it was precisely because, for Matthew, something *had* changed, permanently changed, that his friend's supernatural composure struck him as so suspect.

Clouds drifted across the ceiling. In this new atmosphere of vigilance and expectancy, the *quartier des enfants* swayed to and fro, suspended in a cage. And yet, as before, and at the same hour, on that night and the one after it, Matthew would tiptoe out of his bedroom and along the corridor to Théo's. There, on cue, as though also on purpose, the door had been left ajar, the bedside lamp left on. There he would silently take in the spectacle of brother and sister, their limbs intertwined, one leg visible above the covers, the other's outline just discernible beneath them, like a swan and its reflection on the surface of a lake.

The game was resumed on the second afternoon after that on which Théo had paid his forfeit in kind. They were as usual in the *quartier des enfants*, where Théo, standing at the window, was dreamily following the progress of a tall vertical shadow that slowly traversed it.

Suddenly, just as it formed an X with the pane's crossbar, he clutched at his breast and collapsed on to the carpet.

'Ahhhhh!' he cried. 'They got me!'

Writhing, he tore at his clothes.

'The pain! The agony! Oh Jesus, I'm done for!'

Isabelle finally looked up from her novel.

'What's eating you?' she asked, but incuriously, for form's sake.

Théo immediately sat up again with a grin.

'What film?'

For two days Isabelle had been waiting for him to turn the tables on her. The question still took her by surprise. She could only, stupidly, oblige him to repeat it.

'Name a film, please, in which a cross marks the spot of a murder.'

'Are you serious?'

'Why not?'

'There must be lots of films.'

'Then it shouldn't be hard to name one. You too, Matthew.'

Matthew blanched. Here it was.

'Me?'

'There's no rule says I can't challenge both of you at once.'

'But, Théo, I had nothing to do with what happened.'

'Name a film,' was Théo's answer. 'Or pay the forfeit.'

Vengeance, says a French proverb, is a dish best eaten cold. It was clear that Théo preferred his piping hot. *A chacun son goût*, as the French also say.

Matthew's mind turned over and over to no purpose. If a hope remained to him of deliverance from the consequences of Théo's challenge, consequences on which he dared not dwell, it lay simply in his citing a title. Isabelle, surely, was right. There must exist dozens of films in which a cross is shown to mark the spot of a murder; if not dozens, then a dozen, a half-dozen, three or four; there must at least be three or four.

But because of his fear of what would befall him in this accursed flat, it was no longer possible for him to pull his wits together. Had Théo merely asked him to name a film, any film at all, there too he might have drawn a blank.

Isabelle, meanwhile, had regained her composure. She offered no answer to the question posed her. Nor did she plead, as Théo had done, for some clue or hint. It was she, after all, who had introduced a new dimension into the game and she knew her brother, and she knew herself, too well to be deluded into supposing that either of them could revert to the childish stakes which had once satisfied them.

'Time's up,' Théo finally said in a matter-of-fact tone.

'The film?' enquired Isabelle. It was a mere formality, but one that ought to be respected.

'The film? *Scarface*. Howard Hawks. 1932.'

'And the forfeit?'

'Well now,' declared Théo, sitting up straight. 'I'm not a sadist, Isa, as you know. I'm not even a Sadian. I just want to see everyone happy, no one left out. So I'd like you and Matthew, my two dearest companions, to make love together in front of me.'

Isabelle closed her novel, though not before inserting a bookmark between the pages at which she'd been interrupted.

'As you wish.'

'Not in here, though. I don't fancy sleeping in someone else's revolting spunk. No offence, Matthew.'

While Matthew felt incapable of moving, Isabelle went on asking simple, practical questions as to what was expected of her.

'Where then?'

'In the spare room. In front of the Delacroix. Who knows,' Théo proposed with a smile, 'one reproduction may lead to another.'

'You don't mind if I undress here?'

'Wherever you like.'

She stubbed out her cigarette in a brass ashtray, then walked over to the record-player and started to play the Trenet record yet again. Since the melody had become the game's theme tune, it would have been unthinkable to pay a forfeit without its accompaniment.

She disrobed with no undue haste, as though for sleep. She neither stared ahead flauntingly at Théo and

Matthew nor demurely averted her gaze from them. The one and only vestige of perversity in her performance was that she kept her dark glasses on throughout, removing them only at the end, as though only then displaying her eyes full frontally.

This young woman, who contrived to wear her grandmother's outmoded garments as persuasively as a bird of paradise its improbable plumage, now appeared disembodied, detached from her own torso, which she exposed as dispassionately as though she were holding up for auction a painting of herself in the nude.

It was a fine, slender torso, all of whose folds, dips and hollows were irresistibly tempting to the finger's inquisitive drill – the concavities of the shoulders, buttocks and knees, the shady indentations of the abdomen, the two paths that converge at that magic well deep in the fairy-tale forest of the pubis.

Standing in the puddle of her own clothes, she waited for Matthew to undress in his turn.

For him the moment had come at last, the moment so long dreaded, when he was to be hustled aboard the roller-coaster.

The desire he felt for both Théo and Isabelle struggled

in vain against memories exploding inside his brain with the power of depth-charges, childhood tableaux of schoolboys dragged screaming behind playground lavatories, their testicles smeared with boot polish, their pubic hair shaved. Ridiculous as it would render him in the eyes of his friends, there was but one possibility to be entertained: flight.

He dashed edgeways to the door. But Théo, who until that instant had seemed as indolent as an odalisque, at once leapt to his feet and headed him off. Cornered, Matthew backed away.

A spell had been broken. Théo and Isabelle relaxed. Giggling, they began to close in on him.

'Come, come, my little Matthew,' cooed Isabelle, 'you aren't being very *galant*, you know. Is the prospect of making love to me so hateful?'

'I've seen you!' cried Matthew. 'I've watched you, both of you!'

Théo started back.

'What's that you say?'

'In bed together!'

'Oho,' said Théo, 'our guest has been spying on us. Now that wasn't a friendly thing to do. Especially when we've been so hospitable.'

'What is it you're afraid of?' said Isabelle to Matthew. 'That you haven't any crack? I've always fancied that someone as nice and neat and clean as you might have no crack in his backside, just a smooth full moon of pink, baby-soft flesh. Is that it, Matthew? Is that what you don't want us to see?'

'No, no, no, please, Isabelle, please.'

They pounced on him. Taller, more muscular than he, Théo soon had him on the carpet. They pulled off his sneakers, his socks, his UCLA sweatshirt. In a frenzy he attempted to wriggle from their grasp. Tears sprang into his eyes. A helpless movement of his arm caused it to brush against Isabelle's breasts. Yet, as patiently as though they were peeling the cheeks of an artichoke, as methodically as though they were subjecting him to the torture of a thousand cuts, they went about their executioners' business, baring his hairless, slightly concave chest, his arms frosted with snow-white down, his slim, suntanned legs.

By now Matthew had ceased to offer resistance. Isabelle sitting astride his legs, his arms pinioned to the floor by Théo, he lay there weeping as young children weep, in a welter of tears and snot. He was naked save for a pair of pale blue jockey shorts, which, with a flick of her wrists, Isabelle pulled to his feet and flung in a ball on the floor.

The first surprise was the whiteness of his crotch. Compared to his arms, his legs, his chest, to the perennially bronzed chest of the kind of American adolescent for whom the sun is as simple, daily and nourishing a source of energy as a glass of warm milk, his abdomen made them think of the patch on a wall where a painting has once hung.

His pubic hair was dark, silky and unfrizzy, like that of an Oriental. His testicles were two grey gooseberries. His penis, which was circumcised, was small, almost but not quite abnormally small, and so plump and round as to resemble, rather, a third testicle. A charming thing which, no sooner had one set eyes on it, one felt like tenderly cupping between one's palms like a throbbing little sparrow.

Which is just what Isabelle did. Before Matthew had time to voice a final appeal, she began moulding that penis with skilful hands, a potter's hands, moulding it, sculpting it, glazing it, smoothing its wrinkles.

To Matthew, who had never known the sensation of an alien hand on his sexual organs, it felt as though he had just discovered an unexplored limb of his own. He drew in his breath. Something hard and tight within him, something that had long crucified his soul inside his body, had at last been set free.

When Théo released his arms, they instinctively wrapped themselves round Isabelle's naked shoulders. She eased her body along his, squashing the penis that was now drolly curved like the arm of an Empire sofa and drawing from him another sharp intake of breath.

Their mouths edged closer, then their sexes.

There were still obstacles to be overcome. They were both virgins, Isabelle because she had never made love except to her brother, Matthew because he had never made love except to himself. Eventually, though, mouths and sexes clicked together at the same time, like adjacent buttons simultaneously buttoned on a shirt front.

While outside, below the bedroom window, could have been heard, had anyone been listening, an inexplicable patter of footfalls and a fanfare of police sirens, Matthew and Isabelle gave themselves up to the adorable gaucheries of love. Under Théo's eyes, all at once opaque with self-awareness, they paid the forfeit.

That evening no one tiptoed along the corridor of the

quartier des enfants. If someone had, if Théo's bedroom door had been left ajar and the bedside lamp left lit, this is what he would have seen: Théo, Isabelle and Matthew asleep together, the beast with three backs.

Yet, for all that that first night together constituted a turning point in the equilibrium of the flat, it didn't bring Home Movies to an end. On the contrary, it inaugurated a whole new period of the game. They were now to play it as obsessively, as monotonously, as a shipwrecked mariner plays noughts-and-crosses on the sand, as a convict devises chess end-games with shadows and breadcrumbs. Except that, unknown to them, they were not players at all but pawns, pawns moved from square to square by the real player of the game, who loomed over the board like Fantômas over Paris.

During the two weeks that followed, the sky released sheets of such stinging rain that the trio were obliged to remain almost permanently indoors.

At first Théo continued to make his regular excursions to the sixteenth arrondissement, circling the Palais de Chaillot without dismounting from his mobylette then returning to the flat with the baguette of bread or carton of milk he had purportedly gone to fetch. Before too long, however, even these trips were phased out. The mobylette rusted in the damp hallway.

Clocks wound down and were never rewound. Beds remained unmade, crockery unwashed, curtains drawn. Gradually, the hour of the day, then the day of the week, then the very month of the year, lost its meaning. Weekends came and went unobserved. Saturdays and Sundays – which are, in the well-ordered lives of average, upright citizens, the shining face cards of the social calendar's deck – became harder to tell apart from the faceless number cards of the working week, until the only marker of passing time was a visit to a luxury supermarket in the neighbourhood.

These raids – for such, in essence, they were – left Matthew as panic-stricken as when he'd had to race through the Louvre. While he would fill his trolley with staples, his companions breezily stuffed the pockets and linings of their coats with lobsters, truffles and caviar, mangoes, foie gras, peaches and, on one memorable occasion, a jeroboam of champagne which Théo tucked down the roomy front of his corduroy jeans. The supermarket's exits became for Matthew as nerve-racking as an airport customs hall.

Meanwhile, the cheques which the poet had left for his children lay uncashed on the mantelpiece.

Marooned on this island not two hundred yards from the church of Saint-Sulpice and the Théâtre de l'Odéon, the three young people behaved as any shipwrecked mariners might have done. Once past the initial stage of frantically scanning the horizon for signs of civilisation, of reconnoitring the Palais de Chaillot and even deigning to attend a class or two, they started to resign themselves to what they could all see was destined to be a lengthy sojourn.

When not pilfering delicacies from the supermarket, they would cook and eat whatever foodstuffs were still to be found in the refrigerator. These eccentric decoctions, indiscriminate blendings of sweet and sour, cold and hot, meat and fish, Isabelle served up at table from the saucepans in which she had prepared them. And if either of the men of the house shied from a lukewarm fondue accompanied by an ice-cold compote of broccoli and prunes or an inexplicably mustardy ratatouille, she would declare with a flourish, 'Just eat it as if you're in some exotic country you've never visited before and this is the national dish.'

It was Isabelle who held the outside world at bay. It

was she who, forging her mother's handwriting, wrote a letter to the headmaster of the school she and Théo attended, announcing that both of them were bedridden with viral hepatitis. It was she, too, who accepted to be interviewed by the aunt commissioned by their parents to occupy herself in their absence with their children's welfare.

This excellent lady, who assumed her function of chaperone no more than dutifully, had astounded her family nearly twenty years before by exchanging a violin for a nightclub – which is to say, she had sold the Stradivarius she had inherited from her grandfather, a celebrated Polish virtuoso, in order to purchase a half-share in *Le Nègre Bleu*, a smoky cabaret off the Champs-Elysées. Overwhelmed by invoices, Department of Health regulations and a squabbling staff of hysterical young men, she was delighted to learn from her niece that she and her brother were eating healthily, doing well at school and in bed by eleven.

Little by little, Matthew was granted access to the intimate secrets of his friends. A yellowing photograph, for example, torn from an old *Paris-Match* and squirrelled away by Isabelle inside a tattered copy of the novel by Gide that is titled, precisely, *Isabelle*, of one of the Kennedy sons, in profile, aged fourteen, just after he had been gored in the neck by a bull at Pamplona, and who was blessed, according to her, blood and all, with 'the handsomest face in the world'.

'We hide our blood,' she said, 'when we ought to flaunt it. Blood is beautiful, as beautiful as a precious stone.'

Théo let him examine a page of manuscript that he had stolen from his father's desk and seriously hoped to sell one day for a small fortune. Of the two-hundred-odd words in the poet's handwriting only seven hadn't been crossed out. They were seven words, moreover, that had served as the foundation stone of one of his most frequently anthologised poems.

Isabelle showed Matthew a phial of sleeping pills that she had stockpiled over several months on the pretext of one feigned insomnia or another. These were intended for her eventual suicide, should it ever come to that.

'They're my return ticket,' she said. 'There are born suicides and born non-suicides. The former don't necessarily kill themselves, the latter sometimes do. I belong to the first category, you to the second.'

'I will never kill myself,' Matthew said bluntly. 'I

believe, I truly believe, that if you kill yourself you go to Hell.'

Matthew, too, had betrayed his ultimate secret, the avenue Hoche.

'It's because you're already in Hell that you kill yourself,' said Isabelle.

'That's witty,' replied Matthew, 'but Jesus was wittier. Let me put it this way. I'll never kill myself because I love you.'

'You say that but you may not always love me.'

'I will always love you.'

'I wonder. If *amour* didn't rhyme with *toujours*, maybe we'd never have thought of equating love with eternity.'

Matthew and Isabelle often spoke of incest, of physical love between a brother and sister.

He asked her one day how Théo and she had come to be together the way they were.

'Théo and me? It was,' she replied simply, 'love at first sight.'

'What would you do if your parents found out?'

'It must never happen.'

'Yeah, I know. But what if it did happen?'

'It must never happen.'

'But just let's suppose, for the sake of the argument, that your parents really did find out. What would you do then?'

Isabelle reflected for a moment.

'It must never, never happen.'

There was a pause before Matthew spoke again.

'I suppose, when a mother and father sleep together, you could call that a kind of incest.'

Isabelle burst out laughing.

'Matthew, darling, you're one of a kind!'

One evening, for the first time, Matthew spoke to his friends of his family, his past, his life before the rue de l'Odéon.

'It was two years ago,' he said, 'when my dad came home from Vietnam. He'd lost his right arm. So when we were driving out to the airfield to collect him, we were kind of bracing ourselves, you know, wondering what he was going to look like without it. We all stood there, waiting for him to come off the plane. And suddenly there he was, in his uniform, his buttons shining in the sun. And he looked okay, he looked absolutely fine. His empty sleeve was tucked inside the pocket, the way they do it, and it just made him look sort of casual.

So when he stepped on to the runway we all went forward to greet him. And my mom kissed him and hugged him and she was crying, kind of both happy and sad at the same time. Then my two sisters hugged him. Then it was my turn.'

He paused.

'I was sixteen years old. I hadn't hugged my dad in years. We didn't have any real father-and-son thing between us. I guess I was embarrassed at his being in the service, being in Vietnam. Also, I think he thought I was gay. Anyway, there we were, the two of us, and I didn't know how to handle it. I mean, physically. I just didn't know how to hug him. And it wasn't because he'd lost an arm. I would have felt the same whatever. But I could see that's what he was thinking. And I saw how much it hurt him, how much it humiliated him.'

'What did you do?' Théo asked.

'We shook hands. He held out his left hand and I shook it with my left hand. Then he turned away to talk to somebody else. And that was that. It's strange, though. Because it was only when he lost his arm that I really started to love my father. He would look so vulnerable trying to wash his face or read the newspaper or tie his shoelaces with one hand. It was as though losing an arm had made him a complete human being. But I'd blown it. I had my chance and I blew it.'

The Cinémathèque had been forgotten. They had a Cinémathèque of their own, a Cinémathèque in flesh and blood. Which meant that the game was no longer played merely whenever the inclination seized them. While they read during the day, or played cards, or fumbled one another, the curtain would rise on Home Movies night after night, at six-thirty, eight-thirty and ten-thirty, with matinees on Sunday. The *quartier des enfants* – which was, with routine detours to the kitchen, what the flat had been reduced to – became an echo chamber through which phrases known to every cinephile in the world would waft like smoke rings.

Garance! Garance!

You know how to whistle, don't you?

I can walk, Calvero, I can walk!

It was Beauty that killed the Beast.

Vous avez épousé une grue.

Marcello! Marcello!

It took more than one man to change my name to
Shanghai Lil.

Tu n'as rien vu à Hiroshima.

Bizarre? Moi, j'ai dit bizarre? Comme c'est bizarre.

Ich kann nichts dafür! Ich kann nichts dafür!

Round up the usual suspects.

Yoo hoo! Mr Powell!

Well, nobody's perfect.

Pauvre Gaspard!

Où finit le théâtre? Où commence la vie?

Costumes were improvised, performances rehearsed, scenes that hadn't worked the first time were dropped from the programme.

Rummaging through a wardrobe in the spare room, Matthew unearthed an ancient overcoat that the poet had worn week after week during one of the appalling winters of the Occupation. Its moth-eaten fur looked as though it had been woven out of the pubic hair of a thousand Filipino houseboys.

He threw it over his shoulders. Then, finishing off his costume with one of the cardboard boxes in which Théo stored his collection of *Cahiers du Cinéma*, on one side of which he scribbled a set of simian features, snipping out a pair of holes for the eyes, he made a sensational appearance at the bedroom door in the guise of an ape.

'What film?'

Théo and Isabelle cried out, *'King Kong! Godzilla! The Phantom of the Rue Morgue!'*

Matthew shook his ape's head. His arms dangling at his hips, his back arched, he staggered to the record player in front of which, to the voice of Charles Trenet, he started to dance an obscene shimmy inside the fur skin and the cardboard mask. Then he removed the head. His face was rouged, his eyelashes caked with kohl, his hair powdered with flour. He slowly eased himself out of the coat, underneath which he was naked. Naked, he continued to dance.

Only then did Théo get it. 'Marlene Dietrich in *Blonde Venus!'*

Whereupon, after just a few seconds had elapsed, it became Isabelle's turn to ask 'What film?'

Caught off guard, looking blankly at her and at each other, the two boys shook their heads.

'*A Night at the Opera.*'

When they continued to express bafflement, she pointed at Matthew's circumcised penis.

'Look! Groucho's cigar – Chico's hat – Harpo's hair!'

They collapsed in laughter.

On another occasion Théo happened across a horse-whip that had been stowed inside the flat's lumber room beneath a set of tennis racquets and a complete edition of the Comtesse de Ségur. Draping his body in a sheet, locking the bathroom window and turning on the hot water tap full blast, so that the atmosphere was as humid as that of a Turkish hammam, he spun the whip shoulder-high about his head, like Mastroianni in Fellini's *8½*, while Isabelle and Matthew, nearly invisible in the vapours of steam, scampered in and out of the blistering bathtub to avoid being nicked on the ankles, elbows and buttocks.

With the fleetness of foot of those scene-shifters who soundlessly rearrange the decor of our dreams, one setting would dovetail into the next. The bath, almost overflowing, would become Cleopatra's from the film by DeMille. For want of asses' milk a couple of bottles of the cows' brand were used, the contents of which Matthew poured into the tub, Isabelle opening her legs as wide as scissor blades to receive between them, as in an advertisement for Cadbury's chocolate, the two confluent streams of opaline liquid.

No longer the bedroom's antechamber, a haven for some temporary fugitive from the game, the bathroom now served as an alternative arena for their activities. The tub was big enough to accommodate all of them at once, provided that Matthew sat in the middle to enable Théo and Isabelle, at either end, to encircle his waist with their matchingly long legs, the water-wrinkled toes of the one stretching as far as the armpits of the other. And when Théo pulled down over his ears a canary-coloured Stetson hat which he had been given as a child, a hat once far too large for his head, now far too small, Isabelle and Matthew called out together before he'd even had time to ask them who in what film.

'Dean Martin in *Some Came Running*!'

'Michel Piccoli in *Le Mépris*!'

They were both right.

It was a spectacular Busby Berkeley production number dreamed up by the two young men which constituted the game's masterpiece.

Théo had always had a weakness for the exploding

stars, revolving water lilies and exquisitely garlanded wheels on which that Grand Inquisitor, that Torquemada of choreographers, had broken so many scantily attired butterflies. This, he announced, would be their most ambitious presentation to date, a real *morceau de bravoure*.

Untroubled by how their conduct might strike some unknown, uninvited observer stumbling on their intimacy, tickled at the same time by the absurdity of it all, he and Matthew fetched a gilt mirror from above the drawing-room fireplace, another from the master bathroom, and set them upright against opposite walls in Théo's bedroom.

Exceptionally, Isabelle was barred from attending these preliminaries. But when the rehearsals were over, and everything made ready, she had one of the straight-backed chairs drawn forward for her, as for a parent at an improvised concert got up by her children.

The film comprised two scenes.

In the first, Théo and Matthew appeared before her as Dick Powell and Ruby Keeler. They wore, respectively, a cadet's faded khaki uniform and peaked cap, several sizes too small, and a yellow taffeta dress and cloche hat, both of which had belonged to the children's grandparents. Standing side by side, Théo to the right, Matthew to the left, they began to perform a double striptease. Théo set the ball in motion by untying the ribbon on Matthew's dress, then darted behind him and reappeared on his left so that Matthew, in turn, could unbuckle Théo's belt, whereupon he too would dart round Théo, but this time in front of him – and so it went, from accessories to clothes proper, from clothes to underclothes, with such deftness that Isabelle had the impression of a stage-length line-up of chorus boys and girls weaving in and out of one another, each of them removing a single item of clothing from the next until all of them had been stripped bare.

It was then that they launched into 'By a Waterfall'. Stretched out on the floor, their legs apart, the tips of their toes just touching, their bodies mirrored to infinity, and singing the song as well as they knew how, in spite of forgetting most of the words, they started to masturbate in time with each other. Their penises grew harder and harder, more and more erect, until it seemed as though they too, like their toes, would meet in the middle. At last, arriving at the refrain, with its little falsetto trill, they ejaculated at exactly the same instant, their energies so channelled into their sexual organs that in the fury of the moment the proportions of reality became surrealistically inverted and each was tempted to believe, naked on the floor, that he had been metamorphosed into a giant phallus on whose throbbing vein there stood, bolt upright, a purple-complexioned homunculus spitting gobs of sperm from its tight, lipless mouth.

Applauding madly, Isabelle cried, 'Encore!', a request with which neither of the two performers was able to comply.

So, amid all the laughter and steam, the Trenet record, the unwound clocks, the veiled curtains, the teasing and banter, the dewy, mildewy glamour of a swimming-pool in whose stagnant atmosphere the flat was bathed, the days passed, jubilant and implacable, days divided by nights as two frames of a film are divided by a black strip.

In her mother's name and handwriting, Isabelle dispatched a second letter to the school headmaster, regretfully anticipating a protracted convalescence for her brother and herself, and she and Théo took turns at telephoning their parents in Trouville. The poet, it transpired, had come down with a plaguey flu, most probably something he had caught from his own sickly inspiration. The return to Paris would have to be delayed.

Matthew, too, spun a web of mendacity. He sent off several letters to his anxious mother and father. Since these letters weren't as informative as before, he was glad to announce that he'd been able to move out of his hotel and into an apartment belonging to a famous French author, whose children, as luck would have it, were not only his age but shared his interests.

This unforeseen turn of events thrilled his parents, impressed that their painfully shy son had broken out of his shell and got in with the right sort of people.

The cheques on the mantelpiece had long since disappeared under a mounting pile of books, magazines and comic strip albums, then been forgotten about. Matthew had an overdrawn bank balance provisioned only every other month by a cheque from San Diego. Raiding the supermarket had thus ceased to be a luxury and become a necessity. Unfortunately, the store's detective had been alerted to the trio's presence; and though they counter-attacked by setting up diversions and planting decoys, and once noisily rampaged through the store bearing about their persons only those articles they were prepared to pay for, with the idea of instigating an intervention on the detective's part and pleading outraged innocence after a fruitless search had been conducted, they were soon compelled to acknowledge that the halcyon era of lobster and caviar had drawn to a close.

The kitchen sink was a graveyard of dirty dishes. Shirts, pullovers and jeans boasted an amazing spectrum of stains. Underpants disgustedly rejected days before as beyond redemption were picked up off the carpet, yanked from underneath sofas and armchairs, judged the best of a bad lot and pressed into further service. And because Théo's ragged sheets kept coming loose and catching between the toes of their bare feet, obliging one or other of them to rise in the early hours of the morning and tuck them back under the mattress, they eventually decided to decamp to Isabelle's room.

If this had so far remained off-limits to them, it was out of respect on Isabelle's part for a bourgeois ideal of apple-pie orderliness. Like certain demented housewives who polish and scrub their front parlours to a hallucinatory sheen, so that no one ever dare set foot inside them, she insisted that her bedroom remain untrespassed-on by the others 'in case a visitor calls'. Besides which, it had been convenient for her, whenever occurred one of their ferocious squabbles, to storm out of Théo's room into her own and, biting into an apple as though it were her brother's thigh, bury herself in one of the locked-room murder mysteries on which she doted.

Unhappiness may lie in our failing to obtain *precisely* the right sort of happiness.

Matthew not only loved Isabelle, he was grateful to her for having released him from himself, for having permitted him to spread his wings, where before he had felt beached and impotent, his soul as cramped and pinched and shrivelled inside his body as his penis inside his pants.

Isabelle loved Matthew, but the pleasure she took in making love to him derived above all from the opportunity it gave her to be privy to the pleasure he took in her. She never ceased to wonder at the force with which his head would throw itself back, his distended pupils would float upside-down to the tops of his eyes, his crimped, almondy brown, mild-mannered member would all of a sudden shoot into super-manhood and furiously cast forth its white sap – and this simply by being talked to, like a houseplant.

Both of them loved Théo. Yet, ever since the intrusion

of Matthew, who had entered the life of the flat as one enters a film halfway, Théo had watched him arrogate to himself an ever more prominent place. At first, he had been hardly more than a pet, a tame spaniel wagging its tail at the least sign of affection, an amusing new acquisition to divert Isabelle and himself from their airless intimacy. Now, with the intruder's ascendancy, Théo began to fancy, rightly or not, that he himself had become his sister's lover rather than her twin and that he would henceforth be visited by those anxieties of the lover to which the twin is immune: the pangs of envy and resentment, the torment of sleepless nights spent mulling over what an equivocally worded remark had meant to convey. The knot binding them together had been fatally slackened to include Matthew.

If, as they once had whimsically fantasised about themselves, he and Isabelle had been mythical lovers, Romeo and Juliet, Tristan and Isolde, what were they now? A mismatched couple; or, Tristan and Juliet.

It was now Théo who, night after night, would come padding back from the bathroom, as Matthew once had done, silently pause on the threshold of the bedroom and – resembling, with his alarming eyes and tousled mop of hair, a transvestite whose wig has just been snatched off

– gaze at the two naked, tangled bodies and, beside them, at the crude imprint of his own body on the creased sheet and that of his own head on the pillow, as though he were seeing his own absence, his own ghost.

A taste for vengeance on his part, of an infantile type which he and his sister had exacted from each other since they were barely able to crawl, had brought Matthew and Isabelle together; had, in consequence, like a dull and nagging toothache, exposed him to jealousy, a sentiment he had never before known. It was not, as yet, as though he were truly unhappy: these twinges of his were still too faint and sporadic; just that the happiness granted him could not be reconciled with that which would have been of his own choosing had he been a free agent.

Was it of Matthew that he was jealous? It may have been, rather, that he was jealous, in the word's other sense, of the exclusive hold that he himself had once had over his sister's body and soul. At moments he found himself nostalgic for the purity of the taboo which together they'd breached. That that very purity had been breached in its turn by the insinuation of a third party, however fond he was of Matthew, was a source of obscure distaste to him. There was, too, a quality to their escapades which reminded him of South American transsexuals prowling the Bois de Boulogne by night, of those respectable avenues around the Bois whose pavements are lined by call girls as evenly spaced as parking meters, of orgies organised by middle-aged business executives in hotel rooms with luxuriously stocked minibars and two-way mirrors.

Nor was it of any help to Théo that Matthew continued to wear his heart stitched on to his sleeve. He loved both Théo and his sister the more for having been authorised to love them at all. *I love you.* These three words came to seem as natural to Matthew as breathing. He never wearied of repeating them.

Théo accepted as a right, as something which went without saying, the *I love you* addressed to him. That destined for Isabelle he couldn't hear without a certain gnawing irritation. In this he was more like Matthew than he knew, for what he might have wished for himself was to have had innumerable lovers, for each of whom he would be the one and only lover.

Though these were becoming increasingly rare, there were still spasms of lucidity in the flat, when it would occur to one or other of them that the hour of reckoning was imminent, that the world at large, the world which had indulged them for so long, which had given them their heads, must eventually call them to account. Yet, strange as it seemed (though, truth to tell, they paid no attention even to this strangeness), that hour seemed to have been indefinitely postponed. No telephone call had come from Normandy to announce their parents' impending return, nor had they ever been contacted by their aunt from *Le Nègre Bleu*.

In fact, the telephone had stopped ringing altogether; and once, when Théo picked up the receiver with the project of calling the house in Trouville in an endeavour to forestall the inevitable, he was mystified to find it quite dead, without a dialling tone.

His puzzlement lasted just long enough for him to wonder if he ought to inform the others. Then, assuming that the telephone had been cut off because of a bill left unpaid by their parents' extended absence, he gave it no further thought.

> *Que reste-t-il de nos amours?*
> *Que reste-t-il de ces bons jours?*
> *Une photo, vieille photo*
> *De ma jeunesse.*

Que reste-t-il des billets-doux,
Des mois d'avril, des rendezvous?
Un souvenir qui me poursuit . . .
. . . qui me poursuit . . .
. . . qui me poursuit . . .
. . . qui me poursuit . . .

Like a nervous child stumbling over a multisyllable, the record, frayed from overuse, would invariably catch the needle on the same stubborn groove. Listening to it was an excruciating business. Yet, after a few experiments with other Trenet tunes, or else with popular classics, Sibelius's 'Valse triste', Chopin's 'Tristesse', they all equally felt an urge to return to the number with which the game had originated. And, in the end, the repetition which had once grated on their ears grew to be second nature to them.

They had turned the heating up full blast and would now sashay through the flat in the nude – except that they were never quite stark naked. Each would tend to wear a single item of clothing, which might be: for Théo, a white sheet that he would drape over his shoulders like a toga; for Isabelle, a pair of her grandmother's jet black, elbow-length evening gloves that caused her in the dark to appear armless, like the Venus de Milo; for Matthew, a frontiersman's suede belt worn low and loose round the waist. In this way, they lolled about the *quartier des enfants*, striking a hundred gallant poses a day.

None of them felt the need any longer to refer to the game – if it could still be considered just a game – as Home Movies, or by any name at all, so pervasively had it thread itself into the textures of their existence; and the cinematic allusions with which it had all started, and which its latest evolution had rendered redundant, were eventually dropped. Insufficient now were the playful tugs and tweaks, the giggly cross-dressing, the *touche-pipi*, the goatish adolescent pranks. The props of old had served their purpose, had been discarded, and all that was left was the hard literalness of sexual desire, the skin, the flesh, the body, down into whose orifices, like orphaned fox cubs, they went to earth.

Hunger, though, began to rack their temples with fearful migraines. Wholly without material resources, refusing to entertain the notion of reaching out to either family or friends (for which friends?), they would each in turn cast over their nakedness a dirty, stringy pullover and a pair of stained jeans, tiptoe down into the courtyard and forage in the dustbins that were lined up along one of its walls.

But what they extracted from these, and it was little enough, had the instantaneous effect of constipating them. After a deal of heaving and puffing, along with other, more comical sound effects, they would eventually produce stools that were hard, musky pebbles the shape and colour of miniature rugby balls, causing Isabelle to shriek in agony from behind the bathroom door that she would 'soon have to shit by Caesarean section'.

One afternoon, ransacking the pantry for some edible scrap of food, a crumbling breadstick still inside its cellophane wrapper or a bar of mouldy Swiss chocolate, Isabelle came across a bounty about which she and her brother had forgotten. On the top shelf sat three cans of cat food which had been bought for a recently deceased Siamese.

Théo found a can-opener and screwed open the lids. Then, with their bare hands, they scooped up the moist, jelly-rimmed meat and devoured it without a thought for the future.

Alas, it had on their digestive tracts the contrary effect to the odds and ends they had been rifling from the dustbins in the courtyard. Their faces drained of colour. Their stomachs seethed and fermented with gassy bubbles. Cupping the palms of their hands over volcanically erupting mouths, the three of them made a simultaneous dash for the lavatory.

Isabelle, who had the greatest presence of mind, suddenly switched direction, heading for her parents' bathroom, which was outside the orbit of the *quartier des enfants*, and immediately drawing the lock on the door to repel all boarders.

Théo and Matthew, remaining to fight it out, raced along the corridor to the lavatory next door to Théo's bedroom.

There was a scuffle in the doorway, both of them struggling to keep their bodies from turning inside-out. Yet even if it was Matthew who reached the seat first, he was instantly ousted from it by Théo. Flung backwards, he slipped and lost his balance, skittering across the linoleum floor like a balloon from which the air has been let out, his intestines as giddily aflame as those of a Catherine wheel. Before the eyes of the safely enthroned Théo, his flesh dissolved into a raging, uncorkable torrent of mud, sperm, vomit, egg yolk, soft caramel and silver-flecked snot.

A moment later, when Isabelle entered the lavatory, he was still lying there, stretched out amid the multitudinous fluids that his body had discharged, like a blind man who has stumbled over his own breakfast tray.

Tenderly, she picked him up, sponged him down, poking the bursting sponge into his vaulted crevices, squeezing it out along the sore cleft of his buttocks. Half-acquiescent, half-scared, he let her cleanse him further by shaving off his pubic hair, not only around the penis but along the narrow, smouldering trail of gunpowder which ran between his thighs. Gazing at himself in the mirror, Matthew started to excite himself. He rubbed himself against his reflection. He caressed it all over, but it declined to kiss him anywhere else but on the lips. A faint tracing of these kisses stayed for a while on the misted surface of the glass, before fading away like the Cheshire Cat's grin.

Suddenly, without warning, Théo pinned him against the reflection. Wild-eyed, his nose bent sideways, his teeth scraping the glass, his left cheek flattened against his double's right cheek, Matthew started to gasp for air, so desperately one might have thought his reflection was giving him the kiss of life.

It was obvious that Théo meant to sodomise him.

Previously, between the two youths, a sense of propriety, as to when and where to stop, as to how far to go too far, had always been observed. From its origins, now irrecoverable, lost for ever, their mutual horseplay had confined itself to the petty humiliations and self-abasements of rituals and raggings. Now, with Théo about to rape Matthew, a rape that already filled him with elation even as he knew its intention was to pain and degrade him, they had ceased to obey their own rules.

Silently thrilled by this bizarre new union, Isabelle watched her brother's erect penis squeeze through the narrow, hair-snagged passage between Matthew's buttocks, while, contriving to open a single eye under the pressure of the mirror's reptilian scrutiny, Matthew himself made out a set of scrunched-up features that were his but not truly his, different from his but not truly different. With an agonised moan that could have been either of pleasure or pain, he capitulated unconditionally, assuming at last the role in which his whole life had cast him, that of the martyred angel, frail of physique and lamblike of character, to be caressed and beaten, cradled and spat upon, inspiring in those who are drawn to him and to whom he is drawn a desire to protect, and at the same time a compulsion to defile, the very innocence that seduced them in the first place.

> *Que reste-t-il des billets-doux*
> *Des mois d'avril, des rendezvous?*
> *Un souvenir qui me poursuit . . .*
> *. . . qui me poursuit . . .*
> *. . . qui me poursuit . . .*
> *. . . qui me poursuit . . .*

The household had found the identity it had sought since the morning of the grown-ups' departure. Theirs – Théo's and Isabelle's – was the licence of the masturbator to do, inside his head, whatever he pleases with whomever he pleases for as often as he pleases, a licence that must lead to ever more extreme fantasies. The only difference was that Matthew had become the externalised object of these fantasies. Yet, tormented as he was, subject to whatever indignity they could devise, he also remained the object of his tormentors' love. The indignity submitted to, they would at once tearfully hug him, smother him, suffocate him with kisses, beg his forgiveness with the humblest, the most sincere of apologies.

It was in this alternating current that he rediscovered, again and again, the arousing, demeaning sensations of the avenue Hoche.

The world at large, meanwhile, the world whose average, upright citizens they shunned and were shunned by, the world which came to a halt at the flat's bolted front door as though no longer daring to put a foot inside, that world too, for anyone with eyes to see and ears to hear, was treading air. How else to explain the telephone's stillness, the drum roll of footfalls reverberating from the pavement below the bedroom window then just as suddenly pitter-pattering into silence, the city traversed by ambulance and fire-engine and police-car sirens, criss-crossing one another in the night, traversed as well by what sounded like explosions, even if these were never more than half-audible, like bombs detonated under glass?

And these noises, deadened, anaesthetised, heard as one hears things when cupping one's hands over one's ears before releasing them, these footfalls, sirens, explosions, this shattered glass, this whole end-of-the-world pandemonium, served as an accompaniment to the game's very last phase when, clinging arm to arm, Théo,

Isabelle and Matthew would descend – or, rather, ascend – into Hell.

> . . . *qui me poursuit* . . .
> . . . *qui me poursuit* . . .
> . . . *qui me poursuit* . . .
> . . . *qui me poursuit* . . .
> . . . *qui me poursuit* . . .

The flat was still, silent, sealed as tight as a coffin. The air was fetid. No ray of light pierced the bedroom curtains. Isabelle lay lengthwise on the bed, her head dangling upside-down, her hair brushing the carpet, her feet, as though foreshortened, those of a hanged man. Théo was curled up against her, a lock of lank hair obscuring his eyes. Matthew sat cross-legged on the floor, his head hung forward, his face and breast, like those of a Red Indian, blazoned with crosses, crescents and looping, curling lines, traced out in excrement.

Theirs was no longer the elegant entanglement of a monogram but the ghastly, grey-green quiescence of the Raft of the Medusa.

Nothing could detain them any longer, travellers as they were across a Lethe as polluted as any other river.

Whether dead or merely asleep, they were not to be awakened by any crude, external alarms, not by any of the sirens, explosions, cries, screams, cheers, bowling-alley thumps, screeching tyres, whistles and songs which were none the less drawing closer and closer to them. As in a dream, as in a snowdrift, as in an avalanche of cocaine, the longueurs of eternity had already blanketed each of the occupants of this first-floor flat near the place de l'Odéon.

Then suddenly, like Peter Pan, the street flew in through the window.

A small paving stone, hurled up from underneath, came crashing into the bedroom. It sprayed the bed with fragments of glass. It landed on the record-player. It shattered the Trenet record.

They were not dead.

Through the star-shaped gash in the window bobbed a cold and misty sun. Noise, light and air transformed the room, the noise earsplitting, the light blinding, the air intoxicating.

They opened their eyes. With the gait of astronauts inside an airtight chamber, they unsteadily pulled themselves to their feet. In slow motion they advanced towards the window, drawn to it as though about to be sucked out into space, one foot floating above the floor on which the other would alight with a muffled tread. Théo slipped. Isabelle overtook him. Matthew stumbled into the Empire table lamp. Its bulb exploded without making a sound.

They reached the window. Drawing the curtains apart, Théo opened it and stared down into the street. This, the full length of the narrow, meandering thoroughfare, is what he saw:

To the left, where it led into the place de l'Odéon, amid a débris of rocks, paving stones and lopped-off branches of trees, was a phalanx of helmeted CRS officers, advancing slowly, warily, like a Roman legion. Their leather jackboots crunched on the rubble beneath their heels. In their black-gloved hands were truncheons and riot-guns and metal shields interlocking as in one of those children's puzzles which comprise sixteen little squares but only fifteen movable little tiles. As they marshalled their forces, any gap left by one of them was immediately filled up by another and the metal shields locked into place as before.

Halfway along the street a car had been overturned

and lay on its back as trustfully as a baby waiting to be changed. Ribbed, waffle-patterned iron gratings, like the sections of a Meccano set, had been ripped from the pavement and piled on top of it.

To the right, spilling on to the pavements, flowed a river, a tidal wave, of youthful humanity, arms linked, fists raised in the air, led by an adolescent Pasionaria, a Joan of Arc in a duffel coat, bearing aloft an enormous red flag which fluttered and danced in the breeze.

These young people were chanting as they marched, shamelessly playing to the gallery – which is to say, to the householders who had come on to their balconies and who, after a moment of surprise, of hesitation, started to join in, so that it seemed as though it was the street itself had at last found its voice. And what it was singing was the most beautiful, most moving, popular song in the world.

> *Debout les damnés de la terre!*
> *Debout les forçats de la faim!*
> *La raison tonne en sa cratère*
> *C'est l'éruption de la faim!*
>
> *Du passé faisons table rase*
> *Foule esclave, debout, debout!*

Le monde va changer de base
Nous ne sommes rien, soyons tout!

C'est la lutte finale
Groupons-nous et demain
L'Internationale
Sera le genre humain!

Théo, Isabelle and Matthew were as baffled by the bizarre spectacle that met their eyes as Sarah Bernhardt, who, when her coachman took an unaccustomed route from her *hôtel particulier* to the Comédie-Française, is said to have exclaimed on passing the church of the Madeleine, 'What on earth is a Greek temple doing in the middle of Paris?'

Even if any of them had actually heard the rumour, the Babel, which had progressively supplemented the Trenet record as an accompaniment to the game, it would have seemed to them no less natural than the background music to a film, whose provenance one never thinks to question. What was their amazement, then, to discover that this half-heeded, almost subliminal reverberation was the soundtrack of a whole other film, one of which they were mere spectators, tenuously present, hardly there at all.

It was Théo who roused himself first. 'I'm going down,' he said.

He turned away from the balcony and went into the bathroom to sprinkle his face with cold water. Matthew and Isabelle followed. For the moment no one said a word. They went about their toilet quickly, expeditiously. With his back to the others Matthew scrubbed the occult markings from his face and torso. The excrement, which had dried up and was as hard as mud, flaked off into the wash basin. Then, his San Diego upbringing reasserting itself, he stepped into the tub, unclipped its shower appliance and showered himself all over. Neither of the others did.

They gathered up the clothes that were still heaped on the hallway linoleum, drew on underwear, shirts, jeans, socks and shoes and, still without a single word having been exchanged, ran downstairs into the street.

It had rained all day. Now that the sun had come out, Paris was hanging up to dry. The pavements, the façades of the houses, the raincoats of the CRS glimmered wetly. The overturned car was a red Citroën whose doors had been wrenched off to serve as chain mail. Its windscreen was smashed, its boot caved in. The youthful demonstrators who had been marching to the Internationale squatted behind it in their blue jeans, their scarlet foulards and their two or three layers of pullovers.

The cafés had closed, and chairs and tables had been piled up any old how. Holding glasses of lager or cups of coffee in their hands, their clientele peered through plate-glass windows. Some of them even continued calmly reading their newspapers, reading about just the kind of disturbance that was taking place in the street outside, a few yards away, like those music lovers at the opera who consult the score by the light of a pocket lamp.

In one café a young North African with a gap-toothed smile and a scarred right cheek brutally jerked a pinball machine from side to side. Another man, a native Frenchman, leaning across the bar counter, chatted to the barman who, dishcloth in hand, was rinsing and drying one empty glass after the next with a graceful switch of his wrist. Behind him a coffee percolator was making a louder noise than any explosive.

It was an instant of suspended activity, as at the filming of a battle scene when actors, crew, cameraman and extras await the director's cry of *Action!*

The din, even so, was appalling. In addition to the

cries, whistles and loudspeakers could be heard a whine emitted by the Citroën's klaxon: it had got wedged in by a fan-shaped slice of iron grating. And discernible, too, above all the noise, was a thin, reedy, almost inaudible strain of silence, the silence of suspense, of anticipation, the rumbling silence of the circus drum roll that precedes a perilous feat of acrobatics.

During this moment of respite Théo, Isabelle and Matthew saw everything as though in stereoscopic detail: the CRS with their death's-head gas masks, the litter of paving stones, the crammed cafés, the smoke unfurling from the Citroën's gouged-out windscreen, the householders on their balconies, the head of a child visible through a gap in the balustrade, the demonstrators fanning out in every direction, the red flag borne aloft by the duffel-coated Pasionaria. And the graffiti. For, here, the walls had mouths, not ears.

LES MURS ONT LA PAROLE

SOUS LES PAVES LA PLAGE

IL EST INTERDIT D'INTERDIRE

PRENEZ VOS DESIRS POUR LA REALITE

LA SOCIETE EST UNE FLEUR CARNIVORE

ETUDIANTS OUVRIERS MEME COMBAT

COURS, CAMARADE, LE VIEUX MONDE EST DERRIERE TOI

LIBEREZ L'EXPRESSION

L'IMAGINATION AU POUVOIR

Then the director cried *Action!*

The CRS started to advance. Their truncheons were as pliant in the air as though underwater. The Roman legion was no more. It was every man for himself. Singly or in pairs, gas masks investing them with a Martian otherness, they moved forward, each at his own speed, deflecting with their shields the stones, branches, mudguards and water bombs pelting them from the other side of the Citroën.

At first, briefly, the demonstrators succeeded in standing their ground. A few daredevils among them raised diehard fists. They tried to reprise the chorus of the Internationale, but it petered out in a desultory exchange of cries and jeers. Then, when what little ammunition they had about them was depleted, they fought a rearguard action with whatever else was at hand, stubbing their feet on the street's fissured, treacherously irregular paving and falling down hard on their knees and ankles.

The CRS hurled tear-gas canisters which would land with the thud of a package through the letter-box. After an instant of uncertainty, when no one knew for sure whether they would prove to be operative, there arose out of them small, cone-shaped cyclones of orange smoke. These swelled to monstrous proportions, towering over demonstrators and CRS alike with the uncontainable energy of a genie released from a lamp.

The householders beat a retreat from their balconies, slamming shutters and windows behind them. One after the other, with the gesture of knights-errant snapping shut their metal visors before joining battle, the demonstrators drew foulards up over their mouths and noses. Then they set to running, pursued by the forces of order.

A young black man was cornered by two of the CRS in the doorway of a café. His eyes closed, squeezed tight, his fingers protectively splayed over his short, crimped hair, he collapsed on to the pavement under the blows that were methodically descending on him. From inside the packed café nothing could be seen but truncheons rising and falling, regular as clockwork. Flattening their noses against the glass, those clients who were positioned nearest the window peered downwards in a vain attempt to make out who it might be on the receiving end.

Further off, a young woman in a trenchcoat, very photogenic, very Garbo, long auburn hair tucked under a floppy hat of the same material as her coat, was being chased across the street. She reached an open ground-floor window, passed it, doubled back. At first beneath the terrified gaze of the elderly couple who were framed in this window, then with their active assistance, she plunged headlong over the sill into their flat. Though the window was instantly locked behind her, a policeman's truncheon nonchalantly smashed it in.

Now, eyes streaming from tear gas, the demonstrators darted here and there, two steps forward, one to the left or right, the knight's move in chess, swerving to pick up a stray paving stone and hurl it back over their shoulders, teasing, taunting, changing tack, skidding, falling, carrying the wounded out of the firing range. Meanwhile, diagonally sweeping the chessboard like caped and mitred bishops, the CRS relentlessly drove them on, down the congested street and towards the place de l'Odéon.

It was at the corner of the street that Matthew, separated from Théo and Isabelle in the crowd, tumbled over a semi-conscious young man whose tenebrously handsome features were striped with blood like those of the Kennedy son in Isabelle's photograph. He had lost control of his bladder. A triangular stain was spreading around the crotch of his jeans and down the seam of his left leg.

Confronted with this derelict piece of flotsam, Matthew found himself so moved that his eyes overflowed their banks. An image flashed before them, the image of the ravishing monster he had seen crossing the street in front of the National Gallery. As then, he was impressed by the nobility of this young man, the nobility of his blood-streaked face, his twitching eyes, his foulard, his stained jeans.

Théo's telephone call had awakened him prematurely from his dream. This time, however, it was no dream. He would perform the miracle. He would raise the dead.

He knelt beside the young man, who, mortified by his incontinence, clumsily tried to screen the stain with a limp hand. But Matthew was pragmatic, businesslike. Pulling the young man's arm from his crotch, he placed it over his own shoulders and propped him up against the wall.

'Can you hear me?' Matthew whispered in his ear.

The young man said nothing.

Matthew raised his voice. 'Are you able to walk?' he asked. 'I bet you can if you try, if you let me bear your weight. I'll take you on my shoulders.'

But, as soon as he was standing, the young man's legs collapsed under him and he slid back down on to the pavement.

'Give it all you've got. You can do it. That's good, that's very good.'

Matthew contrived at last to get him into an upright position; and with the young man's hands clasped about his neck, his feet dragging behind him, he started hauling him out of range of the CRS.

He was stopped almost at once by a bearded man in his late thirties. His black leather jacket, beige cotton slacks, open-necked sports shirt and rimless dark glasses identified him as a plain-clothes policeman. His complexion was spotty and one imagined him badly shaved, as it were, beneath his goatee.

Dangling on his shirt front was a camera. He had been photographing the faces of 'ringleaders'.

He shouldered Matthew aside so violently that the blood-streaked young man slithered back down the wall like a cartoon character flattened by a steamroller.

'What the fuck are you up to?' the plain-clothes policeman spat at Matthew.

'Me? I –'

'If you don't want to join pisspot here in the jug, you better fuck off! Now!'

'But, monsieur, you can see for yourself, he's really hurt. He needs treatment.'

The policeman seized Matthew by the lapels of his jerkin.

'Well, well. You're not French, are you? What do you call that accent?' he muttered, clamping him by his neck. 'Deutsch? English? Engleesh?' he said, stressing the adjective to make himself better understood.

'I'm American.'

'American? Well, congratulations, my friend, my Yankee friend.' He gave Matthew a kick on the ankle with his shoe's metal toecap. 'You just got yourself deported. De-port-ed. Capito?'

Matthew wriggled in his grasp. The policeman's nut-brown fingernails gave him goose-pimples. His breath smelt of Gauloise cigarettes.

It was then that Théo magically appeared in front of them. There was a paving stone in his hand. The policeman had no more than a second or two to register his presence before Théo shoved the stone hard into his face. The blow felled him. With a groan he clutched at his nose, blood spurting out of both nostrils at once, his dark glasses dangling from one ear like loose bunting.

Théo pulled Matthew away.

'What about him?' Matthew asked of the young man, who was still lying on the wet pavement. 'Shouldn't we –'

'What are you, nuts?'

Rejoining an anxious Isabelle, they followed the crowd of demonstrators, who were being swept into the carrefour de l'Odéon like a torrent plunging into the sea.

The carrefour was a wasteland. The cars overturned, the buses set alight, the cafés wrecked, the restaurants looted, the last of the wounded limping down side-streets – everything brought home to them the fact that the encounter they had just witnessed had been a skirmish by comparison with the battle of which this scene represented the aftermath.

In the middle of the square a barricade had been constructed. To build it the plane trees which had lined the boulevard Saint-Germain for centuries had been chopped down in a couple of hours. The battle over, lost and won, this barricade straddled the deserted street, undefended, good for nothing but a bonfire.

An old man, wearing a navy blue beret and a black patch over one eye, sheltered in the entrance to the Danton cinema. Fragments of broken glass creaking like snow beneath his shoes, he strained to take it all in. Tears were welling in his good eye. To no one in particular he cried, 'The scoundrels! The scoundrels! These trees were part of Paris's history. It's history that's been destroyed!' He hadn't yet understood that history had also been made; that history is made, precisely, by chopping down trees as an omelette is made by breaking eggs.

Near the metro entrance was a Morris column on top of which, like King Kong, that Quasimodo of the Empire State Building, squatted a pot-bellied young man wearing a pale green windcheater. After several attempts to stand up straight, when he would shakily position himself on an upright footing before dropping back on all fours, he managed at last to retain his balance. As he surveyed the wreckage, one expected him to beat his breast in triumph.

Following their own instincts, Théo, Isabelle and Matthew raced along the south pavement of the carrefour, past the Danton cinema, past the *bouche du métro*, past the Morris column, into the rue Racine. There, the gates of the Ecole de Médecine stood open. Its courtyard was filled with demonstrators who had taken cover like refugees huddled inside the compound of an embassy. Its walls were plastered with mimeographed posters announcing committees and meetings and assemblies; plastered, too, with manifestos, ultimatums and stencilled, scurrilous lampoons of Marcellin, the Minister of the Interior, Grimaud, the Prefect of Police, and de Gaulle.

Borne onwards by the crush, the three friends entered the building.

The atmosphere inside was wayward and fantastical. Medical students scarcely out of their teens strolled along the corridors wearing surgeons' masks to shield them from a tear-gas attack. Above the swing door to the operating theatre some scallywag had affixed a skull and crossbones – not a flag, but a real skull and two real bones. In the basement, in the school's morgue, a half-dozen naked cadavers of frozen, bone-hard flesh were laid out on gleaming trolleys.

In that cold white chamber, these statues of death, these chipped and dusty plaster-casts of death, exposed to obscene commentaries and unflinching stares, would have appeared dead even to the dead. They were riddled with death, as a dying man may be riddled with cancer. Not even Christ could have revived them.

A discussion was being conducted around the cadavers. If the school were to be besieged, should they be carried out into the courtyard and hurled over the gates at the CRS?

There existed, to be sure, a magnificent precedent in the Cid, whose corpse, strapped to his saddle, led the Spanish army into battle against the Moors. But no one knew what to do. No one dared take a decision. The young iconoclasts drew the line at the dead.

An hour later, news having arrived that the CRS had turned off along the boulevard towards Saint-Germain-des-Prés, the students who were not on duty that day, whose names were not posted up in the occupation roster pinned on to a bulletin board in the school's central hallway, sneaked into the street and made their way home.

Having chosen not to inform themselves for fear of being ridiculed, Théo, Isabelle and Matthew also thought it wise to slip away.

The absence of passers-by, of traffic, endowed the carrefour de l'Odéon with a draughty film-set vastness. On every side, along its tributaries, the rue de Condé, the rue de l'Ancienne Comédie, the rue Hautefeuille, in twos, threes and fours, bleeding or unhurt, demonstrators were tiptoeing off the deserted stage on which the drama had been enacted. There was, too, at the last, one young boy in a voluminous cape who momentarily interrupted his flight so that he might gather up, with the mischievous pirouette of a periwigged blackamoor, a bloodied red foulard which a fellow fugitive had let fall in the gutter.

That same afternoon, to their surprise, the place Saint-Michel had been spared. Even so, only one of the brasseries around the fountain was still open for custom. As they walked past it, their intention being to cross the pont Saint-Michel to the Ile de la Cité then recross the Seine by a bridge further south, someone inside the brasserie rapped on its window.

'Théo! Théo!'

It was Charles. A year older than Théo, he had formerly been his classmate, until they had lost contact with each other when he entered one of Paris's polytechniques as a student of economics. Even at school, his politics had been conservative and capitalist. He read the *Wall Street Journal*, for which he had been obliged to place an order with a bemused newsagent, and he would airily allude to 'seeing my banker' when all he meant was 'going to the bank'. But in a cynical world he was not a cynic. Théo was very fond of his starchy, old-world gallantry, his flapping arms and the silent laughter that would shake his tall, broad-shouldered frame.

They went inside.

Charles was standing alone at the window holding a glass of lager. He was unrecognisable. Instead of the parodically sober dark suit which had long been his trademark, he wore a leather bomber jacket with a filthy fur-trimmed collar, a pair of mottled jeans and a loud plaid shirt. Even more extraordinary was his head, which had been shaved all over, except for a thick top-knot in the Chinese style.

He slapped Théo on the shoulder.

'I don't believe it! Théo! How's life?'

For a moment Théo didn't know how to respond.

'Charles? Is it you?'

'What do you mean, is it me? Of course it's me. Don't you recognise me?'

'You, yes.' Théo pointed at the topknot. 'That, no.'

Charles gave it a tweak.

'Don't you like it? Don't you think it suits me?'

'I don't understand.'

'What don't you understand?'

'You,' said Théo helplessly. 'Always so chic, so well-dressed. Double-breasted suit, polka-dot tie, *Wall Street Journal*. Now look at you.'

Charles looked instead at Théo.

'You've changed quite a bit yourself, you know. You stink, for example.' He fingered Théo's clothes. 'And what's with the rags? You look like something out of Zola.'

'It's a long story,' said Théo after a pause.

There was a still longer pause, until, with a grin, Charles replied, 'So is mine.'

Then, kissing Isabelle and shaking hands with Matthew, whom, being no cinephile, he was meeting for the first time, he added, 'Let me buy you all a drink.'

They asked for food instead.

'Food? Well, I wonder,' said Charles, glancing at the bar. 'There's a shortage, after all. But I'll see what I can do.'

They didn't understand what he meant by shortage. But there were so many things they didn't understand.

A few minutes later, when he returned with sandwiches and Coca-Colas, Théo put the question to him again.

'So? The topknot?'

'I've been living in Mongolia.'

Charles visibly savoured the effect which his revelation had on his friend. He wasn't disappointed.

'Mongolia!'

'I spent seven weeks in the Gobi Desert with a nomadic tribe.'

'But your studies? The polytechnique?'

'Oh, my studies . . .'

He gazed blankly into the middle distance as though those studies belonged to some dim, defunct and irretrievable period of his life.

'Look about you, Théo. History, knowledge, imagination – they've taken to the streets. They're in circulation.

They're no longer the private property of an élite.'

'I didn't know,' said Isabelle, 'that the *Wall Street Journal* was delivered in the Gobi Desert.'

'I don't read Fascist rags.'

Théo and Isabelle were confounded by this impostor.

'What's happened to you?' cried Théo.

He gaped at the survivors of the battle, now drinking beers and Cokes as though taking a break between tutorials. 'What's happened to everyone? Why are there these barricades, these CRS vans everywhere? What's going on, for Christ's sake?'

'You're seriously asking me that question? You really don't know?'

Charles examined Théo's features for a hint that he was being teased.

'No! No, I tell you.'

'Where the hell have you been?'

'Away . . .'

'Away? How did you get back in?'

'Back in?'

'How did you re-enter the country?'

There was no answer to that. His eyebrows raised like two bushy circumflexes, Charles returned Théo's own blank stare.

'I'm beginning to think it was you who were in the Gobi.'

Persuaded at last that, for a reason he could not as yet fathom, his friends knew nothing of the upheaval which had convulsed the faculty of Nanterre, then the whole of Paris, then 'the four corners of the Hexagon', as newsreaders like to say, he began to relate to them the legend of what was already coming to be known as *les événements de mai*.

And so it was they learned how the expulsion of their own Henri Langlois from the Cinémathèque had been the Sarajevo of these *événements*; how, at the very least, that expulsion had crystallised a spirit of revolt that was already in the air, had served to light a flame that was to be relayed from hand to hand like an Olympic torch.

'It's not just the university, not just Paris!' said Charles, who was no longer able to contain his lyricism. 'The whole of France is on strike. Phones don't work, banks have closed, there's no post, virtually no petrol left. It really is a general strike, students and workers united, a common front against a common enemy. A new society is waiting to be born, Théo, a new world! A world without *grands-bourgeois* and *petits-bourgeois*, *grands-fascistes* and *petits-fascistes*. A world that'll no longer have any need of the old world's tired old masters! No more Leonardo! No more Mozart! No more Shakespeare!'

He paused.

'No more Hitchcock!'

'Never!' cried Théo.

There was another pause.

'You'll see, my friend,' Charles murmured softly. 'You'll see.'

Paris was a carnival. Michel Foucault was headlining at the Maubert-Mutualité amphitheatre, Sartre at the Sorbonne, Jean-Louis Barrault and Madeleine Renaud, sharing the stage with their own public, at the Théâtre de l'Odéon. Queues formed early, good seats were at a premium and it was often standing room only.

Old ladies on the sixth or seventh floor poured basins of water on to the heads of the CRS, then closed their windows and drew their curtains with a speed and a zeal that belied their age and respectability. Fretful mothers hovered in the wings of demonstrations until, spotting their teenaged offspring, they would cuff them on the ear and drag them home, deaf to the immemorial objection that their pals had been permitted to stay. Nor were these teenagers the very youngest of the militants. Following the expulsion of a pupil from the Lycée Condorcet, the schoolchildren of Paris had elected to call their own strike. Downing fountain pens and wooden pencil-boxes, they paraded through the streets of the Left Bank alongside their elder brothers and sisters. 'What next?' fumed an indignant leader in *Le Figaro*. 'Are we to expect tots from the primary schools to rise up in revolt?'

Charles then mentioned a young German, Daniel Cohn-Bendit.

This Cohn-Bendit was nicknamed Dany le Rouge. He represented the street. He spoke to the street and made himself its spokesman. He charmed the street as Orpheus charmed the beasts. Wherever he went, the street followed him.

The street had always come timorously to a halt on the thresholds of houses. Now these same houses invited it in. The street entered. It made itself at home. And the day would come, said Charles, the day would come when the Assemblée Générale would be besieged by all the streets of Paris and Dany le Rouge would make his entrance borne shoulder-high by his court of streets, his cortège of streets, radiating from him as from some human Arc de Triomphe.

Théo was struck dumb. The country had been turned inside-out and he had had no intimation of it. And he understood now why no telephone call had come from Trouville, why the poet and his wife had failed to return, why their aunt from *Le Nègre Bleu* had ceased to trouble herself with their well-being, why they had been able to live for so long in a misrule of isolation and disorder.

As the café had become stuffy and overcrowded, they decided to leave. Slanted rain drummed on the pavements, causing their bodies to bend like those of circus clowns on weighted shoes.

'You all need to be re-educated,' said Charles, adding mysteriously, 'Come to Maspero with me.'

'Who or what is Maspero?' Isabelle asked as, cupping her hands against the flame, she lit her last cigarette in the wind.

'You *are* Martians, you three. Come with me, I'll show you.'

Maspero was only a few yards away, in the rue Saint-Séverin. It turned out to be a bookshop, over whose front door could be read *La Joie de Lire*.

Inside, its walls had been plastered with as many manifestos as those of the Ecole de Médécine, along with stencilled posters of upraised fists clutching bombs and roses. In pride of place, however, were three silk-screen portraits, of Che Guevara, Mao Tse-tung and Ho Chi Minh.

With his symmetrical features, which did nothing more than fill in the blank spaces between his jet-black curly hair, his black beret, his thick black eyebrows and even thicker black beard, the first of these recalled a Rorschach blot. The second had the shiny, enigmatic countenance of a eunuch. The third, with his mandarin's cheekbones and beard, suggested one of those quaint figures which, if inverted, reveal another, slightly less convincing face, as in a Rex Whistler caricature.

La Joie de Lire was patently used by its customers as a library rather than as a shop. Its well-thumbed stock, strewn across table-tops or shoved into white wooden bookshelves, was being consumed by the same young people – leaning against its walls or sitting on its uncarpeted floor, none of them contemplating making a purchase – who had been demonstrating in the streets an hour or so before. Even the bookseller, his feet stretched across the counter, his chair tipped back as far as it could go without toppling over, was imperturbably reading Rosa Luxemburg.

In one corner stood a group of Latin American students. You knew they were Latin American by the sultry maestria with which they affected to wear their berets *à la* Che, by their hobnailed boots with leggings as complicated as sailors' knots and by their revolutionaries' granny glasses. They smoked minute cigarillos which hung wet and skewed from their lips, gave off a peppery aroma and had to be relighted after every puff. Sporting Zapata moustaches as bogus as those scrawled by children on billboards, they liked to think of themselves as political exiles. Yet nothing could have been more absurd than their camouflage fatigues.

Charles started picking up books off the tables as mechanically as though he were shopping in a supermarket. These books were tough little objects whose lurid black-and-red covers made one think of tiny revolutionary tracts. They would have disturbed the patrician serenity of the poet's library. He would have rejected such cheap paperbacks with the art collector's scorn for reproductions.

'Read these,' said Charles. 'Maybe then you'll understand how and why the world is about to change.'

Isabelle turned them over in her hand.

'Where's *Das Kapital*? Shouldn't we be cutting our teeth on *Das Kapital*?'

'*Le Capital*' – for Charles, a true initiate, the work already existed in his own language – 'is the Bible. One of the greatest texts ever committed to print. But it's far too difficult to start with. You have to earn the right to read it.'

'How are we to pay for these?' Théo asked. 'We're broke, or hadn't you noticed?'

'Take them. Everyone does. Pay for them when you can. If you can.'

Leaving the bookshop, they strolled along the boulevard Saint-Michel, over which hovered a pall of ashgrey smoke, uncertain in which direction to drift.

They talked. Rather, it was Charles who talked.

Were its naïve faith in the insurrection of the masses to be transcribed in detail, his discourse would sound banal. Yet it wasn't banal, because to speak of changing the world is itself a means by which are changed those who speak of it. And, without truly being aware of what was happening to them, Théo and his sister found themselves once more in thrall to a cause, a charm, an exciting new drug. For the addicts that they were these terms had become synonymous.

As for Matthew, his eyes, like those of the Madonna of the avenue Hoche, were open but seemed closed, too closed for a sounding of their depths to be taken.

It was exactly half past four when they arrived at the Drugstore in Saint-Germain-des-Prés. At that hour, it presented an oasis of warmth and light on the grey boulevard.

'Lend me some money, will you,' said Isabelle to Charles. 'I want to buy cigarettes.'

The Drugstore was squeezed in between a chemist's shop with its green, neon-lit cross and a *café tabac* outside which was affixed what looked like an inverted red fire-extinguisher. In front of its glass-enclosed terrace, inside which young waiters in tartan blazers served banana splits and Pêche Melbas, a group of male prostitutes, dressed in the latest fashion of the oldest profession, furtively or blatantly patrolled their beat.

They crossed the empty boulevard.

While Isabelle went off to buy her cigarettes, the others entered the Drugstore. To their left, stairs led up to a restaurant whose tables were laid out around a small, circular gallery overlooking the ground floor. On its walls were enormous pairs of lips sculpted in bronze – of Bardot, Deneuve, Elsa Martinelli. Further left, another staircase led to a second, almost identical restaurant. Beyond, a third flight of stairs descended to a lower-ground-floor shop which sold gadgets designed to soothe jangled nerves: a row of steel balls attached to a pulley which clicked pleasantly, one against the other, when set in motion; a rectangular glass casing mounted on a hydraulic frame and filled with mercury, in which, at the pull of a lever, Hokusai's wave was animated before one's eyes.

Even if the view from the enclosed terrace was obscured by a fleet of CRS vans parked along the boulevard, the Drugstore's clients consumed their cheeseburgers, salades niçoises and osso buccos as though nothing were amiss, as though it were any other month of May but this. The men wore Italian jackets gashed by deep vents in the back and open-necked shirts with frilled cuffs and broad, pointed collars folded flat over their jacket lapels. When one of them stood up, a miniature gold crucifix would catch the light. The women wore bracelets, charms, bangles, necklets and earrings which made the Drugstore resonate with the tinkling of cowbells in the Alps.

Charles studied them all with loathing. He already saw them facing a firing squad, crucifixes ripped from their necks, cowbells silenced for ever. 'These are the *petits-fascistes* I was talking about,' he muttered. 'Fit for nothing but the dustbins of history.'

When Isabelle rejoined them, Théo asked Charles if he could put them up for the night. Without articulating their unease, they knew they couldn't return so soon to the flat near the place de l'Odéon, the flat that, until that morning, had been sealed off from the outside world.

He agreed without posing either questions or conditions. He warned them, though, that he was going home only to shower and change. He was to be at the place Denfert-Rochereau at six o'clock. The faculty of Nanterre having reopened, its students had decided that their victory, however short-lived it might prove to be, should be celebrated with a demonstration covering Paris in its entirety. That day's exchange of fire had been one of the preliminary bouts.

The plan had been to march to the television studio to denounce its coverage of the insurrection, then onward to the Palais de Justice in silent protest against the parody of law and order that had left scores of their fellows in prison cells. But the Prefect of Police had at once taken the step of confining all demonstrations to the ghetto of the Latin Quarter. If by such a stratagem he had hoped to remove the sting from their protest, he couldn't have been more mistaken. The injunction was interpreted as an appointment, an appointment Charles meant to keep at Denfert-Rochereau.

He lived close to the Eiffel Tower, in a third-floor, two-roomed flat which he rented cheaply because, being in the well of a courtyard, it was as sombre as a basement. Théo had dossed down before in the spare room on whose floor mattresses were laid out as in a dormitory. It had just two other pieces of furniture: an illustration from a novel by Jules Verne, enlarged and framed, of a bearded man with pince-nez standing in the luxuriantly sylvan grounds of a crystal-domed observatory and pointing, for the benefit of a younger, beardless man at his side, to a crescent moon of unusual luminosity, with the caption *La lune! dit le docteur*; and an aquarium of such impenetrable obscurity that its occupants (always assuming there were any, for they were invisible) could imagine, because Charles had been too preoccupied for several weeks to change the water, that they were swimming in the ocean's most turbid depths.

It was a little after five-thirty when they arrived at the flat. Having forgotten how hungry they were, they raided its refrigerator, devouring salami, cheese, a bowl of radishes. Preparing to take his shower, Charles glanced back at his trio of guests.

Matthew was seated in a corner of the room, his chin grazing his knees, his upper lip crested with a marbly white streak as though he'd been drinking milk from a carton, his lower lip the sort of wavy line a child might draw to represent a gull in flight. Isabelle lay flat out on Charles's own unmade bed, matching forelocks framing her features like a Pollock's theatre curtain, her eyebrows two black feathers. Théo was slumped in a great soft beanbag of a chair.

'By the way,' Charles finally said, 'where *have* you been?'

At first no one spoke. Then Isabelle answered. Making precisely the same gesture as the astronomer it depicted, she pointed up at the Jules Verne illustration.

'There. On the moon.'

By early evening, at half-past six, demonstrators converged on the place Denfert-Rochereau and started to clamber over the lion of Belfort.

Crying 'Free our comrades!', they marched the length of the boulevard Arago, passing the Santé prison, from whose barred windows inmates, none of whom were likely to be students, waved invisible handkerchiefs at them.

At the intersection of Saint-Michel and Saint-Germain a road block had been erected by the CRS. It denied access, on one side, to the place Saint-Michel and the bridges of the Seine, and on the other to the boulevard Saint-Germain, forcing the demonstrators to spill out on to the rue Gay-Lussac and the place Edmond-Rostand, which jutted from the boulevard like the nose of that dramatist's most celebrated hero.

In the course of the evening the occupation of the Latin Quarter got underway. With the majority of demonstrators hemmed in by the CRS between Edmond-Rostand and Gay-Lussac, others stealthily infiltrated the neighbouring streets and squares, the rue Saint-Jacques, the rue du Panthéon, the rue de l'Estrapade and the place de la Contrescarpe. The first of the barricades, too, were erected, out of railings, gratings and paving stones.

By ten o'clock an intricate labyrinth of such barricades stretched from the place Edmond-Rostand to the rue d'Escarpes, and from the intersection of the rue d'Ulm and the rue Gay-Lussac to the Lycée Saint-Louis. Unfortunately, these barricades, which on a map could have been mistaken for bridges, were exactly the contrary of bridges. The idea was that, like a ship's bulkheads, if one of them were to cave in, the others would succeed in limiting the damage. But the effect was rather to frustrate the possibility of flight, since they also had to serve as arsenals. Were the onslaught to come, the demonstrators, possessing no more sophisticated weapons of attack than the gratings and paving stones which also constituted their sole means of defence, would have to rob Peter to pay Paul.

On television, at quarter past eleven, the Prefect of Police, a bouquet of microphones thrust into his face, patiently explained that he himself had once been a student, that in his youth he too had taken blows from police truncheons and that he could therefore understand and even sympathise with the students' motives. But there was a limit, after all, and when all was said and done.

Then, in a direct address to the demonstrators themselves, employing one of those euphemisms grimmer than what they are supposed to soften, he stated that, if the Latin Quarter hadn't been evacuated by midnight, he had been instructed by the Minister of the Interior to 'clean it out'.

At half-past twelve the Maginot Line of barricades was as entrenched as ever and the Minister's instructions were passed on to the CRS.

Into this ravaged landscape, one paradoxically both lunar and moonlit, one that, from a bird's eye view, crisscrossed by its barricades, resembled nothing so much as a chessboard, came Théo, Isabelle and Matthew.

From Charles's flat – he himself had left home two hours before – they had walked along the quays of the Left Bank, along the quai d'Orsay, the quai Voltaire and the quai de Conti, until they had turned into the rue Saint-Jacques, at the foot of which they stood together for a few minutes. It was saturated with tear gas. Its street lamps wore mauve haloes. Its houses, shuttered, incurious, felt as unfamiliar to them as those of a city, a Zürich or a Barcelona, to which they were paying a visit for the first time.

Advancing towards the battle, they saw, ahead of them, Zeppelin-heavy clouds of smoke in a blood-red sky. Whenever a flare shot up and fell back to the earth in a spill of cascading sparks, it would spotlight, as though for their sakes alone, some act of individual courage and self-sacrifice: a young girl beating with her fists the chest of a policeman who had smashed the knuckles of her male companion; a middle-aged house-holder in cardigan and slippers rushing down into the street to help a group of demonstrators overturn a car, perhaps his own.

They continued on their way.

Somehow, miraculously, darting from the left pave-ment to the right and back again, ducking inside empty, unoccupied doorways, sprinting through streets and squares, Théo forging ahead, Isabelle and Matthew try-ing to keep pace with him – as, so long ago, they had sprinted through the corridors and salons of the Louvre, as though that race had been the dress rehearsal for this one – they reached the barricade in the place Edmond-Rostand. Under the cross of another chemist's they flat-tened themselves against a stained mattress which was propped up on wooden crates and out of which wisps of white wool protruded like tufts of white hair inside an old man's ear. As they crouched there, a trellis of shad-ows rimmed the smoky infuscation of their eyes.

The light from the CRS torches spattered the walls, the barricade, the faces behind the barricade, with stars, haloes, snow-blots. Here and there, an image, the fragment of an image, a mere detail, privileged at random, stood out, a gaping mouth, a crudely bandaged forearm, a surreptitiously exchanged kiss, a finger pointing – but why? at what? at whom? Sounds were heard, a grating laugh, a cry of 'CRS-SS! CRS-SS!' or 'De Gaulle Ass-ass-in! De Gaulle Ass-ass-in!', but heard as though badly dubbed on to a film's soundtrack.

Hours passed or seemed to pass.

Three, four, five times, the CRS attempted to breach the lines, only three, four, five times to be driven back. Tear gas canisters winged over the barricade and visors were drawn up. Householders opened windows high above the demonstrators' heads, throwing down towels for their protection, fetching basins and jugs, filling them up and returning to their balconies to pour the contents into the street, for ice-cold water is known to attenuate the effects of tear gas.

Near the barricade behind which Théo, Isabelle and Matthew crouched, and under a street light which cast a halo at her feet, a young black woman was being subjected to interrogation by a trio of CRS officers. While the other two blew into their cupped hands and flapped their arms against their sides to keep warm, one of them would shove her repeatedly against the railings of the Luxembourg Gardens. Whenever the young woman's head struck a railing, all three would count out in chorus, ' . . . *et trois . . . et quatre . . . et cinq . . . et six . . .*'

Incensed, provoked beyond forbearance, she finally pulled off a glove and with her long, lacquered fingernails engraved four parallel scratches down her assailant's cheek, scratches so profound they could be seen, or nearly, from the barricade on the opposite side of the square.

The CRS officer squealed in pain. Gingerly, he drew a finger along the scratches and inspected the beadlet of blood on its tip. Bellowing 'Salope!' at the young woman, he gave her a vicious jab in the abdomen with his riotgun. Staggering, shrieking, whimpering like a tortured animal, she lurched forward on to the pavement, one netstockinged leg upswung at a freakish angle atop the other, like that of a cat performing its toilet.

This was too much for Théo. Oblivious of the rockets, flares and canisters overhead, he stood up and rushed

over to the scene. At the very last minute the officer
brusquely turned his head. Théo thrust his knee into the
man's crotch, hard enough for him to feel it jellifying
under his kneecap.

The officer's face decomposed into a piece of crum-
pled waste paper.

Then, fatally, Théo hesitated. He couldn't decide what
to do next. He ought to have run the gauntlet of the rue
Médicis or else sought refuge inside one of the houses
behind him or shinned over the railings into the Luxembourg Gardens to make his escape by its south gates.
Instead of which, he continued to stand rigid, the living
embodiment of Zeno's paradox, waiting, almost expect-
ing, almost begging, to be apprehended by the two
policemen who were only yards away from him and
who, an instant later, had him prostrate, his palms
swallow-cupped on his crotch.

At the sight of their truncheons hammering her brother's body, Isabelle clutched her face in her hands. No
longer caring to what hazards she would be exposing
herself, she quickly picked her way along the top of the
barricade, stumbled, fell, grazed her knees, her ankles,
the backs of her hands, slid down the other side and ran
to his aid.

Now Matthew was alone. His heart pressed on the accelerator, tore ahead, out of control. He struggled to collect his wits. A diversion, he said to himself. His friends were being hurt, were being beaten. What was needed was a diversion.

He looked frantically through the enveloping shades, searching for a weapon, for a prop of some kind.

Suddenly he noticed, on the ridge of the barricade, that a red flag, planted between two oblong slices of iron grating, had been knocked over by Isabelle. Unattended, it lay flat, inert, across the paving stones.

He remembered the duffel-coated Pasionaria. This memory gave him the courage he already possessed. He would once more raise the flag. He would create a diversion so that Théo and Isabelle might flee to safety.

Without further hesitation, he scaled the barricade, lifted up the flag and swung it high above his head. Then, failing to understand that the word *Fin* was advancing towards him like a train emerging from a tunnel, he started to sing.

> *Debout les damnés de la terre!*
> *Debout –*

A shot rang out.

Brandishing the flag, Matthew turned into his own statue.

On the far side of the barricade, a CRS officer stared in disbelief at his machine-gun. He held it at arm's length and seemed only just to have realised that it was loaded. He pulled off his tear-gas mask. In spite of this mask there were tears in his eyes.

'I couldn't help it!' he cried. 'I couldn't help it!'

Matthew turned aside from him and fell forward in a heap.

Fighting free of their captors, over whom the shot appeared to have cast a spell, Théo and Isabelle ran to where Matthew was lying, knelt down on either side of him and cradled his head.

He opened his mouth. His tongue hung slack on his lower lip. It was flecked with foam.

In his contorted features they could read the terrible truth that one not only dies alone, one *dies alive*.

He tried to speak.

But, even in death, Matthew would remember too late, much too late, what it was he intended to say.

Though, as we grow older, we have fewer reasons for hope or happiness, fewer of those which do remain to us will turn out to be illusory.

It was a dry evening in early October. A squally wind having blown up from the Seine, the roller-skaters' Coca-Cola bottles spiralled off the Trocadéro esplanade as skittishly as flat pebbles over a river. The Eiffel Tower sparkled like a neon sign.

That evening the Cinémathèque was so crowded that the *rats* who had failed to find unoccupied seats were authorised, just this once, in defiance of fire-hazard regulations, to sit wherever there was room, on the flight of steps leading down into the auditorium, along the aisles, on the carpet under the screen's vertical vastness. As for those who had arrived altogether too late, they continued to throng the foyer and the staircase, forlornly toying with the praxinoscopes and the shadowboxes and the magic lanterns, hoping that a seat might even then become vacant for them, that someone already seated might be seized by an epileptic fit.

Thwarted by concerted protests, protests which had been amplified by the events of the spring, de Gaulle had finally been obliged to reinstate Langlois as the

Cinémathèque's curator. Those two national institutions, Henri Langlois and the Cinémathèque Française, had been reunited.

When Langlois walked on to the Cinémathèque's stage, the whole house rose to its feet to acknowledge the prodigal's return with a spontaneous ovation.

He introduced François Truffaut and Jean-Pierre Léaud, the director and star of *Baisers volés*, the film to be presented that evening *en avant-première*. They too were applauded. Then, the lights dimming, the curtains parted reluctantly from their embrace.

To everyone's amazement, the film opened with a shot of the avenue Albert-de-Mun and the path running parallel to it into the garden of the Cinémathèque. Superimposed on this shot, in Truffaut's own handwriting, was a dedication: '*Baisers volés* est dédié à la Cinémathèque Française d'Henri Langlois.' The camera then slowly panned towards the Cinémathèque's entrance, closing in on the padlocked grille and the sign *Fermé* attached to it. A salvo of applause greeted the allusion and a ripple of emotion swept through the auditorium. Some members of the audience rose to their feet as before and cheered. Others wept.

On the soundtrack, as the credit titles unrolled, the voice of Charles Trenet was heard:

> Ce soir le vent qui frappe à ma porte
> Me parle des amours mortes
> Devant le feu qui s'éteint.
>
> Ce soir c'est une chanson d'automne
> Devant la maison qui frissonne
> Et je pense aux jours lointains.
>
> Que reste-t-il de nos amours?
> Que reste-t-il de ces bons jours?
> Une photo, vieille photo
> De ma jeunesse.
>
> Que reste-t-il des billets-doux,
> Des mois d'avril, des rendezvous?
> Un souvenir qui me poursuit . . .
> Un souvenir qui me poursuit . . .
> Un souvenir qui me poursuit . . .
> Un souvenir qui me poursuit . . .
> Un souvenir qui me poursuit . . .

Had the needle stuck?

If it had, it was for just two members of the audience.

They were seated in the very front row and, as they listened to Trenet, their eyes glittered like those of their neighbours. Their tears, however, when they came, welled up from quite another source.

Afterword

The first version of the novel you've just been reading was published in 1988 under the title *The Holy Innocents*. It was my own first novel, one with which, although it received a good press on the whole – a few reviewers were ecstatic, a few were dismissive, most were in-between – I was at the time of publication, for several reasons, profoundly dissatisfied and remained so ever after. So much so that when, almost at once, my agent received a proposal from a film company, I told him categorically to refuse it. And when, over the years, producers continued to show interest, I asked that I not even be kept informed of who they were and what they were offering. (I am, in this one sense, a yes-man, in that I tend to find it easier to say yes than no.)

My agent respected my request until the spring of 2001, when he finally caved in. He felt (rightly, as it happens) that I would wish to know not just that an offer had been made by Jeremy Thomas, the most adventurous and least parochial by far of contemporary British film producers (*Merry Christmas Mr Lawrence*, *The Last Emperor*, *Crash* and so forth), but that it had been made on behalf of a filmmaker for whom I had an enormous admiration, Bernardo Bertolucci.

I accepted the offer and also accepted Bernardo's and Jeremy's suggestion that I myself screenwrite the adaptation: the offer, because I couldn't think of a single filmmaker in the world who struck me as having a greater affinity with the novel's themes than Bernardo; the suggestion because it gave me an opportunity concurrently with my screenwriting assignment to rewrite – or rather, as in a palimpsest, to *overwrite* – that first version with which I was so unhappy. (There was equally the fact – let's be honest – that I stood to make a lot of money.) The new, changed title, *The Dreamers*, was mine, but the impetus to drop the original came from Bernardo, who cared for it as little as I myself had come to do. It was to be the first of innumerable changes.

Bernardo's film now exists. If the reader has already seen it, he or she will realise that this book, although much closer to the film than the first version, is not at all what is termed a novelisation. That is deliberate. And perhaps I can explain why by way of a whimsical little analogy. If one wears dark grey trousers, let's say, and a jacket which is also grey, *but not exactly the same grey*, the result looks awkward and inelegant, almost as though one were hoping to pass the ensemble off as a suit. Far better to wear a jacket in a different colour altogether. So with a novel and its cinematic adaptation.

So, too, with my novel and Bernardo's film. They may be twins but – just like my own fictional siblings, Théo and Isabelle – they're not identical.

G.A.

April 2003